Finally, though, I couldn't stand it any longer. I put my arms around him and kissed him. He was shaking, almost as if he were afraid. But he responded right away, mouth coming open, drawing my tongue into him, pushing back with his own...holding me so tightly it was almost as if he were clinging to me for...for something more than an exchange of sexual expression. He was still trembling, and even the solid hold we had on one another didn't seem to alleviate it...not for quite a while. Then, he seemed to respond more to me than to whatever it was that troubled him. He began unbuttoning my shirt, and I did the same with him...

Also by LARRY TOWNSEND:

beware the god
who smiles

LARRY TOWNSEND

BADBOY

First BADBOY Edition 1995

First Printing September 1995

ISBN 1-56333-321-X

Cover Photograph © 1995 Charles Hovland

Cover Design by Dayna Navaro

Manufactured in the United States of America
Published by Masquerade Books, Inc.
801 Second Avenue
New York, N.Y. 10017

Chapter 1

MASTEN, Gregory K.—File No. 42366. Admitted May 8, 1970, on Authority San Ramon P.D., following attempted burglary Museum of Antiquities, 433 Front Street, that city. Patient suffering obvious paranoid delusions at time of admission. Violent. Sedated, Rx 334-B. Assigned neuro-psychiatric, for observation and recommendation. Phys. descr.: Ht—6' 0", Wt—175 lbs, Hr—Blond, Eyes—Hazel, Age—(est.) 20. Ident. mks: encircling scars both wrists and ankles, small circular scar (brand?) left hip, extensive bruises and contusions, cervical back to buttocks.

When Dr. Paul Lawrence came to work on Monday, May 11, the Masten file was on his desk, along with those of several other patients admitted to the psychiatric unit over the weekend. There were always several of these at the start of each week. Most of them were juveniles or young adults, picked up by the police or sheriff's department for being under the influence of hallucinogenic drugs—that, or an occasional drunk suffering from the D.T.s. The Masten case was different. It rang an alarm in Dr. Lawrence's head.

The doctor shuffled a second folder from his drawer of active cases: O'CONNER, Kenneth P., age twenty-four, guard at the Museum of Antiquities...admitted two weeks before with the same kind of marks on his body, also classified violent—though this had not happened until he realized he was to be hospitalized. He was originally reported nude, lying on the floor of the museum, in an apparent state of catatonia. He reacted only when another guard attempted to remove him.

Miss Gleason interrupted the psychiatrist's thoughts with the usual pot of coffee and a sweet-roll from the commissary. She placed the tray on Dr. Lawrence's desk and stood waiting for him to break his reverie and look at her. She had entered without knocking, which always annoyed the doctor; but Miss Gleason was an old-timer at the hospital—old enough to be his mother, if that dried-up officious body had ever been capable of bearing children.

"Good morning, Doctor," she said brusquely.

"Good morning, Nurse," Dr. Lawrence forced a smile.

"I see you're looking at the Masten file," she observed dryly. "Have you checked your appointments?"

The doctor sighed. "No, but I suppose you have me booked solid," he said. The hint was lost on Miss Gleason.

As she read his list of duties, Dr. Lawrence munched on his breakfast roll. He made no comment until she finished.

"Now, let's see," he replied at last. "I want to have a little session with this new patient—Masten, so we'll have to change a few things around." He went down the list, recalling each item from memory...the time, the patient. His easy use of intelligence exasperated her, the casual display of unassuming superiority a seeming reminder of her own short-comings. And in most things, Miss Gleason was anything but inadequate. "I think we can let our intern handle the routine ward rounds on his own," the doctor continued. "It's about time we gave him a chance to make some decisions."

He paused, then, thoughtful, almost pensive, his soft grey eyes gazing in unfocused concentration. "What do you think, Ruth?" he asked.

She melted a little at that, couldn't help it. When he used her first name it implied a type of intimacy, made them co-workers on a footing of mutual respect. "You mean about turning Dr. Gold loose on his own?" she asked.

"Oh, no...no. I'm not worried about that. No, I mean this O'Conner case, and now Masten. What do you think?" he asked again.

"O'Conner is hallucinating," she said firmly. "Any man who imagines himself under the spell of an Egyptian idol..."

"I don't know," mused the doctor softly. "There's something more..." His eyes moved to fasten on Miss Gleason's nose. *All it needs is a wart*, he thought. "No, there's something more than a classic case of paranoia. O'Conner's recall is so vivid...consistent. And the marks on his body. That's what really bothers me, I guess. The man has scars—not just cuts or bruises, but scars, as if he'd worn irons for weeks or months…" He shook his head. "I just don't know; and now we have Masten. I'm almost afraid what I'm going to hear from him."

"You surely don't believe all this nonsense!" retorted the nurse.

"It isn't a question of believing it," replied the doctor slowly. "It's that I can't explain it. I can't supply an adequate alternative."

"Well, of course, I haven't seen the entire file," suggested Miss Gleason hopefully. She tried not to sound huffy, but she had been left out and she didn't like it.

No, and you aren't going to see it, thought the doctor. "That's true," he mumbled quickly. He made no other comment.

Obviously, the doctor wasn't going to let her read his notes or listen to his tapes. Ruth Gleason sniffed and glanced at her watch. "Well, if Dr. Gold is going to make your rounds, I'd better find him and get him started," she said.

At ten, Dr. Lawrence interviewed Gregory Masten. The patient was under restraint in a private room—what used to be called a "padded cell." He appeared haggard and emotionally drained, but otherwise calm and rational.

"When can I get out of here, Doc?" he asked.

"Are you sure you want to?"

"Of course! Whatta'ya mean, 'Do I want to?'"

"I mean you have a felony charge hanging over your head," said the doctor gently. "You might be more comfortable here than in the county clink."

"I can get bail if you let me out of here," Masten

said. "And I can beat the burglary rap." A handsome boy, he suddenly jerked his head to stare at the doctor with his wide, brown-speckled, greenish eyes.

Paul Lawrence regarded his patient thoughtfully, not unaffected by the display of youthful innocence. "Sit down," he said, "and let's see if we can get a few answers."

In his interviews with O'Conner there had been mention of a young man named Greg, who answered Masten's description. Dr. Lawrence was sure it was too close a fit to be coincidence. Phrasing his sentences so as not to threaten or frighten his patient, he began a careful questioning. He obtained enough that first day to bring him back the next…and the next. Much to his amazement, he eventually obtained a pair of stories that fit…fit much too well for each patient to be written off as suffering classic, paranoid delusions. From the beginning, Dr. Lawrence took tape recordings during his interviews with each man.

He hated to admit it, but the two cases were becoming an obsession with him, mostly because neither adhered to any proper, diagnostic pattern. There was also the tantalizing tendency for each man's story to corroborate the other. He began going over his notes and listening to the tapes at night, when Miss Gleason had gone home. He found himself peculiarly affected…and aroused…drawn by what he heard.

Chapter 2

(Started with some encouragement from the doctor) Okay, Doc, as long as you guarantee me this won't go any further, I'll tell you the whole story. You're a psychiatrist, so I guess nothin' a guy does is gonna surprise you very much.

See, the Museum of Antiquities is a private outfit. All the stuff belongs to Walter Silverman, and I guess you've heard of *him!* He's sort of what they call a "gentleman anthropologist," among everything else. He's got a bunch of degrees, and he's been all over the world collecting these things. The biggest part of the collection…at least the part that's attracting the most attention right now, is the stuff he brought back from Egypt just over the last couple'a years. See, when Nasser decided to build that big dam at Aswan, he

11

gave permission for any qualified scientists to dig in the area that would be under water after the dam is finished. Whatever they found they could keep. And Mr. Silverman hit the mother lode!

There's a lotta small artifacts, like necklaces and little statues and a few coins. But the most important thing is a big, black stone-carving of a god. And there's a kind of argument about this, you see. Silverman says it's a primitive idol of Anubis. That's the old god of death, sort of…an assistant god to Osiris. But other people say it's Seth. He's the god of evil. But Silverman says it was found too far south be Seth, because not many idols were built to him in what they call "Upper Egypt." Worshiping Seth was kinda like worshiping the devil, at least to the people who lived in that area. Further north, some of the invaders had idols to him, but that was way up in the delta.

The idol has an animal's head, though, you see; and they can't decide if it's a jackal—that would make it Anubis—or a donkey, which would make it Seth. What really confused 'em all was that the damned thing seemed to have a Mona Lisa smile, and I guess the Egyptians didn't make their gods do that very often.

Silverman found him in a small, underground tomb—not far from Abu Simbel. Along with him there was the mummy of a man, and a couple skeletons as if two guys had been buried in the tomb alive! All this stuff, including the skeletons, is in the Egyptian room.

Now, I'd worked there about six months, and I'd gotten used to all the spooky business of being alone with the contents of a tomb at night, and all. It didn't bother me any more. I came on duty a couple of hours before closing, and I stayed all night—slept in the back after midnight rounds. The other guard, Sam Fischer, came on at eight and opened the place at nine-thirty. Well, this one afternoon there's a young guy in the museum when it's time to close. He's been there about an hour, and...well, I know there's nothing unusual about it. Anyway, this kid...about twenty, taller than me with a great build and handsome as hell, blond.... Anyway, he's been looking at me, and I been looking at him.

So, when it comes time to close—I was all by myself that day...when it comes time to close, I asked him if he'd like to stay a while, and he says "sure." There wasn't anybody else around, so I just locked up the front door and joined the kid—Greg, he said his name was.... I joined him in that Egyptian room. He was standing in front of the big idol, just kinda looking it over...real fascinated by it, 'cause I'd seen him staring at it earlier.

I sat on a corner of the stone sarcophagus behind him, and we rapped a while about the exhibit. Then he turns around and looks at me, big kinda greenish eyes staring into mine without sayin' anything; but I knew what he was thinking, and I was groovin' on the same channel. He walks up to me, standing real close so his legs're between my knees and my face is about even with his belly...real slender waist, and he's wearing dark blue Levi slacks with a low rise through the crotch. There's a heavy, round bulge in the center, like he's wearing jockey shorts and there's not enough room for everything he's got...really turned me on!

So I rub my hands along his sides and over his hips, around to the front where I can feel it all warm and hard...really hot and ready, man...curved around in there like it wants'ta jump out and stand up for me. I sort'a cup my hand underneath his jock, and I look up at him, and he's staring down at me. It's gettin' dark, because I haven't put on any lights and the sun's setting outside.

"Isn't there some kind of sexy light?" he whispers. "I want to watch you."

Wow! This kid's really got me started, and as it happens there's two oil lamps built into the base of the idol. See, this god is sitting down like they usually are, staring in front of him with his hands on his knees, holding a kind of scroll between them. The bottom part of the statue is a big, square block, all carved outta the same piece of black rock. Only this one's got two places by the feet where you can pour in oil and it makes a pair of lamps. I saw Dr. Silverman fill 'em one day, and I knew they worked. So I get up and I strike a match, and I light 'em. They make a deep red, flickering glow, dancing all around beside the god's feet. And because the tomb musta been forgotten, or lost before it could get robbed, the idol still has the original rubies in its eyes. These sort of sparkle and shine, like they're staring right at us. Weird, man! Real weird, and that's where I think the trouble started. Not right then, but it led to what happened later.

So I go back to where the kid's standing, kinda turned to watch me, but still between the sarcophagus and the statue. He's got one hand down by his crotch, and he's strokin' it, slow-like, lookin' at me and waiting. Only now, his cock's about to tear through the cloth, curved up and out like a coil-spring. He's unbuttoned his shirt, so I slip my hands inside and feel that warm, smooth skin. He's got a hard little belly-button and a washer-board stomach…tanned copper-color like blonds'll get. But in the light from the gas lamps it looks more like the reddish gold on some of the stuff from the tombs.

He steps back after a few minutes, so's his butt is touching the base in front of the idol. Then, while I'm watching him, he slowly opens his belt and runs the zipper down his fly so his cock's shoving the white shorts out though the V. He rubs his hand across the material and looks at me with a crooked, cocky smile. "You want it, man?" he whispers. "You wanna swing on it?"

He shoved his pants and shorts off his hips, so the little narrow band of white shows about his waist. And this big cock comes soaring out…man! It was a long, wide hunk'a meat, sort of flat from top to bottom, but thick from side-to-side. And it looked mean—I mean wicked, like a gnarled old oak stump, with heavy veins and a head like a big, ripe plum! I wanted it, all right; but I knew the kid was going to tease me, and I wasn't quite ready to beg him…not quite. So I let him stand there, playing with himself while that cock got bigger and harder, and I could feel my mouth watering for it.

"Take your clothes off," he says suddenly. "If you're gonna swing on this," he say, "I want you kneeling in front of me like a naked, fuckin' slave!"

Well, I've gone this master-slave route, Doc. I'll admit it really flips me. And this kid's got such a really unbelievable cock, and I'm so hot by now…. So, I strip…just stand up and peel…everything. And a'course my cock's as hard as his—not as big and thick, but it's standin' up 'til it almost lays flat against my belly. I can see the kid watchin' it, still smiling his

15

wise-ass smile and fingering that flag-pole between his legs.

When I'm all the way naked he pushes himself up a little, so he's standing straighter. His legs are spread as wide as he can get'em with his pants down around his knees. "Okay," he say, "chow down, man! Let's see if you can cop my joint and get all of it down your gullet in one, big, juicy gulp!"

Well, I went down on my knees and I took it…I mean, I took it like I was gonna swallow a sword. It was down my throat until it wouldn't go any further, and I still lacked about an inch. Then the kid grabs my head and he shoves me hard—all the way, so's I feel my guts pull up and I'm tryin' ta choke and heave. But that big hunk'a meat's got everything cut off. I can't suck air in, and I can't cough anything up! My eyes are shoved into his crotch, against all that curly hair like corn-silk, and my shoulders are pressed tight on his legs.

Finally, he lets go my head, and I pull back from his tool. It's shiny and slick, and my throat aches, and I can taste the gorge in the back of my mouth. My slobber's running off his cock, but it's so hard and ready! The kid starts to reach for my head, and I don't make any move to resist him. Then he changes his mind, like some funny thought's struck him. "Turn around. Put your back to the statue!" he says, kinda laughing. "Let's make a sacred ceremony out of this."

Well, I figure he's just a screwy kid. Guys get funny ideas when their balls are all riled up, sometimes, so I do what he tells me. I crawl around so my feet are flat up against the stone, and when I lean back my ass and shoulders touch it, too. Then the kid steps up between my knees, and he grabs the back of my head and he shoves his cock down my throat again. Then pretty soon he starts pumping his hips, really pounding it into me, and I'm playing with myself...not hard, though, 'cause I'm so fuckin' close I'd shoot my load if I really started wangin' on it.

Then, while the kid's fuckin' the shit outta my mouth, he starts mumblin' something. At first, I think he's talking to me and a'course I can't do much except just roll my eyes to look up at him. I can see his lips moving, but he's not lookin' down. His eyes are set on a row of hieroglyphs, carved into the scroll the statue's holding in its hands. The crazy kid is reading the inscription. I already knew he was a student from the university, so that part didn't surprise me; but it was real wild!

There I was on my knees, my back to that big, black idol. The oil lamps are burning behind me, sending up tongues of flame that made shadows of red and black keep flickering across this kid's belly and what I can see of his chest. And while he stands there, shoving my head against his crotch, and fuckin' me with that outta-sight cock'a his, he's reading all the ancient writing...and I guess he's pronouncing it like it's written—not translating it, I mean, 'cause I can't understand what he's sayin'. Sure wasn't English, anyway.

Then, about the time he finishes reading it, he starts to pop. He's got my head shoved against him with both hands, and I'm almost ready to black out 'cause I can't breathe and I can't hold my breath much longer. Then I start to shoot, too, squirtin' it out all over the floor. His cum is pouring into me, and my face is buried in his hair so my nose is almost flat and I can't hardly open my eyes. Still, it seems kinda strange, because I was sure I saw lights flash…like a bluish streak of lightning. But like I said, I was almost ready to pass out, and with my eyes pushed in his groin like they were, it could'a been because'a that—you know, like when something presses on your eyeballs you see color…. Only…

(Some encouragement from the doctor) Only the kid…he saw it, too! See, he's rolling his hips and givin' me the last of his load…and he's got his eyes closed, too, he says. Only it's like this blue light is flashing and he looks, and for a second everything's so bright he's blinded. Then it's dark, and he figures he's imagined the whole thing. I tried to stand up, but Greg's holding my head and he won't let go…makes me stay here swingin' on his joint until it's all-the-way soft…big and thick, but soft. Man! Doc, I'm sorry, but it's givin' me a hard-on just to talk about it! I hope you're enough of a psychiatrist…I mean, you seem sort of young, so I hope you've heard…

Chapter 3

Dr. Lawrence re-wound the spool of tape and placed it in its box. *So far, so good. Nothing in that first session except two men engaged in a simple—certainly not uncommon— sexual act. Nothing unusual, unless all these mystical trappings…. Ridiculous!* Again the doctor sat back, chin cradled between thumb and forefinger, trying to find a rational explanation where there was none. Much to his chagrin, he had been ready to write off O'Conner's case as a particularly vivid set of delusions. This explanation had not satisfied him; yet, he had no justification to hold the man while he pushed for deeper causes. Now there was Masten. *Of course, O'Conner's initial experience came first. Masten claimed his was later. Could O'Conner have somehow planted the seed of his own hallucination by telling the boy about his "experience?" Unlikely, but it seems to me I remember something in the literature…parallel delu-*

sions…think that's what they called it. What else had they said about the condition….

He pulled out the second tape and placed it on the player. *There's got to be a clue in all of this. Must be something beyond all this erotic rambling, and if I can control my own responses to listen for it…* The doctor grinned to himself, feeling the warm glow in his own crotch. *But if a guy could really experience this—whew!*

Tape File No. 674: O'CONNER, Kenneth P.

Where do you want me to start, Doc? (Where we left off last time.) Well, I donno. If I tell you this, you're going to be sure I'm nuts. You'll never let me outta this place! (But it happened, didn't it?) Oh, man…I donno anymore. It seemed so real…. (Just tell me how you remember it.)

Okay. So I finish with the kid, and he finally lets go of me, and I stand up. He kinda grins at me, makes some remark about how sexy I look all naked and hairy with the flames reflecting off my sweat. He digs that, see. Runs his hands over my shoulders and chest, wiping the moisture against me so the hair is plastered to my skin. Then he pulled his pants up and says he's gotta leave, and will I let him out. All of a sudden he's in a hurry!

Well, I am awful sweaty…and naturally I don't have a towel or anything right there. So I figure, what the hell? It's dark outside, and the museum's set back on a big lot with all kindsa trees and bushes around it. Nobody's gonna see me. I just leave my clothes there and I take Greg to the side door. I haven't put on the burglar alarm, yet, so I just open up to let him out. He pauses a minute and stares at me. I'm bare-ass naked, like I said, and the kid looks me up and down, comes up and puts his arms around me and kisses me. Man, he holds me against him so...I donno, it's...wild... wild! Here I am, standing in the doorway with a cool breeze against my butt, and this tall, groovy kid is holding me, kissing me, shoving his tongue down to my tonsils so I'm starting to get hot again.

"Can I come back?" he asks finally. "Later, I mean?"

"The place is open to the public," I tell him.

He smiles and I smile. "See'ya," he says, and he walks away down the path. I stand there in the doorway a couple'a minutes, 'til I start to feel a little chilly. I close the door and I make sure it's locked. Then I walk back to where I left my clothes. Now, Doc...I swear, now...I haven't had anything to drink, and I don't ever drop pills or blow pot...nothing!

So, I walk into the Egyptian room and I start to pick up my clothes. They're all helter-skelter, near the corner of the sarcophagus, some things on top of it, the rest on the floor between it and the idol. I'm standing there, trying to untangle my shorts...still bare-ass naked, when I happen to look up at the god. The flames are still burning in the lamps at its feet; but they're lower now, and the fire makes more shadows than light across the chest and face. But the eyes... those two big rubies that make its eyes...they're burning a deep, hot red. At first I don't react, but then it comes to me. There isn't any light strong enough to reflect like that! There's hardly any glow from the hall, and nothing from the windows. It's just the two oil lamps, and they keep flickering. I guess I must have taken a step closer, and then...that's when something really happened, or when something knocked me out and I dreamed the whole mess!

While I'm standing there, holding my shorts and staring up into the idol's eyes, the arms...the big, heavy arms that aren't even carved so they're free of the god's sides...they start to move. The left one comes toward me with its palm turned open and up. The right one raises to the side, pointing; and the head turns so it's facing in the same direction. And man, I don't mind telling you! The hackles were up on my back, and I could feel the hairs trying to stand up on my head. Scared? Scared isn't the word for it! I wanted to turn around and run, and all I could think about was Lon Chaney and that fuckin' mummy in the case behind me, and I knew it was going to climb out any second and come after me.

But that never happened. And I couldn't run. It was like my feet were in some kind of machine that moved me where the god was pointing. See, there was a big display case over there, built partly into the wall, part extending out across a table...all covered by sheets of glass that joined to form a sort of irregular-shaped "L." Inside this was a reproduction of the area where the idol and the mummy and most of the other stuff was found...reconstructed the way Dr. Silverman thought it must have been when the tomb was built...and sealed.

There were little figures of people coming out of a temple built into the side of a cliff, and the Nile in the distance with boats—feluccas, I think they called them—and more little figures working on the wharfs. Then, in the foreground, but to the side is a small burial complex being built. Pharaoh—this is sort of a smaller, less prosperous Pharaoh from one of the early periods—he's being carried by slaves on his golden litter, and he's pointing to the stones as if he's telling his architect something he wants done. It's all very realistic, and it was the thing I liked best in the whole room. I'd been coming in to look at it, standing there for a long time almost every night.

Well, that's where the god was pointing, and that's where whatever it was that held my feet was taking me. And as I got closer two things happened at once...and all much faster than I can tell you about it. First, the whole display case starts to turn lighter and lighter, like the neon is coming up...only it's not. And while this is going on something takes hold of me... not like a man's hand or anything, but sort of like a plastic shell that's molded to my body. It seems to fit all across my back and shoulders and arms...and against my head, because I'm being pushed forward and made to bend. My face is getting closer and closer to the glass...and then I'm there! I'm really there! I'm kneeling on the sand, and it's burning hot, and the sun's shining up above, and priests and soldiers are standing all around me. And Pharaoh's riding by on his golden litter, waving a bushy-tailed wand at everyone, sort of like the Pope blessing the crowds.

It's dry and dusty, and suddenly I'm thirsty. I don't know why, but I have the feeling if I turn around I'll be back in the museum room. So I try it, and there's nothing holding me any more. Only there's just more desert behind me, and long lines of slaves pulling ropes to haul a great big block of stone up the side of a sandy slope. I only have a minute to think about it, but it comes to me that all the slaves are short, hairy men—like me. The masters...the Egyptians are smooth-skinned, some pretty dark, but without any hair showing at all. Most of 'em are naked except for a short, linen shirt and a headdress. Then someone talks, only I don't realize at first he means me. He's not speaking English, but I can understand him.

"Hide your eyes before the radiance of Nebnotes," says the guy.

I turned around, and here's a pair of soldiers—tall, slender studs with kilts made of a coarse material, like bleached gunny sacks—and they've got long spears with sharp bronze points on 'em. In back of them is a man in a long, white robe, with embroidery down the front and a fancier cloth on his head...and a big, jeweled collar around his neck. He's the little figure of the High Priest come to life! I don't know what to do, so I just stare at 'em, until one of the soldiers swings the blunt end of his spear and cracks me along-side the head.

I kinda fall forward, then, and the other one shoves his foot down against the back of my neck so's my face is pressed into the sand. And it was like being dropped on a griddle, let me tell you! Damn near seared the skin right off me! "This is one of the slaves who dese-crated the floor before the gods," says one of the soldiers.

"He is unmarked. To whom does he belong?" says a real stern voice. It had to be the priest, but I still couldn't see anything.

"He looks like one of the northern barbarians," the soldier tells him. "He must belong to Pharaoh."

"Hyksos!" spat the priest contemptuously. "They are an ignorant and stupid people. See to it he is branded and put him back to work with the others. Our gods seek no vengeance for the acts of unenlightened savages!"

I'm so confused by all of this, and still can't believe it's really happening, I don't try to say or do anything. The priest walks away, and the two soldiers bend down to grab me by either shoulder. They drag me to my feet and start shoving me toward the place where the slaves are tugging at the ropes. Then, one of them laughs and says something to the other…something too fast for me to understand. They stop, and both of them are looking at my cock.

"He is uncut!" says one.

"Even the Hyksos circumcise their sons," says the other.

"But the Hittites do not!"

Suddenly, instead of holding on to me, both of 'em step back and poke the tips of their spears against my sides. "Hold your hands behind your head!" says one. Then they march me up another slope, to a small pavilion where the guard captain is layin' on a couch, watching down the other side of the hill where his men are moving along the lines of slaves. He's got two young guys waiting on him, one holding a long pole with ostrich feathers on the end, fanning him. The other's just standing to one side, next to a small table where there's wine and goblets, and food, I guessed.

The soldiers shove me to the open, front-side of the tent, sticking me in the ass with their spears until I'm almost under the over-hang of cloth. Then, one of 'em grabs me by the hair and shoves me down on my knees.

"What's this?" asked the captain.

"He appears to be an uncircumcised spy, sir," said the man directly behind me.

"He has already desecrated the altar of Anubis," said the other.

The captain looks me up and down, and nods. "Has the priest seen him?" he asks.

One of the soldiers kind'a chuckles. "When the High Priest saw him, the barbarian was kneeling with his face in the sand…"

"As he should have been," remarked the captain.

"But in that position, one could not see…this," said the man beside me. He lifted my cock with the point of his spear.

The captain regarded my pecker for several seconds without saying anything, and the soldiers waited with their spears poised to skewer me if I moved. I was still too confused to know what to do. There wasn't any place to run, if I did get loose, and I kept thinking I must be asleep and dreaming it. I even pinched myself; but it was real. It was real, Doc!

I was there, kneeling in front of this officer, the bottoms of my feet sore as hell from walking in the hot sand. I could feel the sun burning my back and ass, sweat rolling down my face, my sides…throat so dry I could hardly swallow. I didn't—I don't know how or why…all I know is I WAS THERE!

Finally, the captain gestures for one of his boys and tells him to "get Paneb." The boy runs off down the hill, and the officer looks back at me. "Why don't you tell us who you are?" he says.

"I…" I shrugged helplessly. "I'm not a spy," I said. "I'm just a…a traveler, and…"

"What language does he speak?" asked the captain.

"It is not the tongue of the Hyksos," said one of the soldiers.

"No, he is not the desert people," agreed the captain. "But I do not know the language of the Hittites." He looked at his two soldiers.

"Nor I," says one.

The other shook his head, too. "No, but I have heard the Hittites speak, and it sounded much the same."

"Listen," I tried to tell them, "I don't know any of this Hyksos or Hittite crap, but I'm…"

One of the soldiers cracked me with his spear, and about that time the kid comes back with another man. This guy's wearing a kilt and headdress like the other soldiers; but he's bigger and heavier, with muscles bulging all across his chest and arms. And he's carrying a mess of heavy, brass chains and fasteners in his hands.

"Bind him" says the captain.

I start to get up, but both soldiers jammed their spears into me. The guy with the chains—Paneb—he comes around behind me and fastens one set on my ankles. Then he looks at the captain. "Is he to be put with the other slaves?" he asks.

"It will be necessary to question him first," says the captain.

The guy grunts some kinda answer, 'cause I guess he'd of chained me differently if I was goin'ta work. He pulls my hands behind me and chains 'em; only there's too many links between my wrists to satisfy the officer. By putting one hand all the way behind my back, I would have been able to stick the other out pretty far in front of me. "Use a neck band," says the captain, and the guy slips a leather collar around my throat and attaches the middle of my wrist chain to it.

"Do you know the language of the Hittites, Paneb?" asks the captain.

"A few words," says the big guy. He speaks gruff, but he's real courteous to the officer.

"See if the slave will respond to you."

The big guy talks to me in a funny-sounding language that I don't understand. When he finishes, all the others are watching me, so I just tell them in English that I don't know what he said.

"He speaks a dialect I have never heard," says the big guy.

The captain and Paneb—who I think was called Keeper of the Slaves—stand talking for a couple of minutes, while I kneel there with the two spears stuck in my ribs. Now, it's a funny thing, Doc, because with all the trouble I'm in, and solid as everything is...I mean it's REAL! I still have the feeling it can't be happening. And the idea of being chained like this...well, the only time I've ever had restraints on me before was...was for sex. Just a couple of times, I played that way...and...I can't help it, but standing naked like I was...in the warm sun, all chained up.... Well, shit, I started to get a hard-on...not a full, stand-up thing, just kinda half-way, so's it hangs out more than it should, long and sort of arched outward from my balls.

The captain tells this Paneb to take me...someplace. I didn't understand where, and the big guy looks at me. I can see his eyes on my cock, and a grin comes over his face. That only made it worse, 'cause I feel my prick jerk a little and stand out even further.

He grabs hold'a the chain down the center of my back and pulls me up—shoves me along a path, down the back side of the hill. I can feel the hot sand under my feet again, and the path's rocky so's I flinch and almost stumble. Paneb doesn't say anything, just keeps his hold on the chain, and helps to balance me. The weight of his arm is pulling back on the collar, though, so there's pressure against my throat…and I can't help it, but it's turning me on more all the time. I can feel my balls swinging against my legs, and my cock's waving half-hard and I'm naked and the sunlight's so warm all around me…

Then we're inside a tunnel. It's at the bottom of the hill we've just come down, and it's a long, narrow passageway cut right through the rock. Once we're past the front it's black as pitch until Paneb lights a torch. He used a couple pieces of flint or metal; I couldn't really see. But the torch was greasy and it caught right away. Now he gets in front of me, hooks a finger through my collar and pulls me after him. The passage musta been an old one, 'cause the floor was all worn smooth and I could see a heavy, crusty coating of soot and smoke all along the ceiling and top sides of the walls.

Paneb leads me down a fork to the left, and the tunnel cuts lower all the time until it's cool and musty-smelling. It never got damp, though—seemed it should have, but it didn't. Then we're in a big, hall-like room…huge place, carved out of rock and lined with ten, maybe twelve stone gods down each side. There's a light at the end, and Paneb snubs out his torch on the floor.

He turns to me and grins. "You are Amix?" he asks.

"No…no," I stammered. "My name is Ken," I told him. "Ken…"

"You need not pretend with me," he says. "You are among friends."

"Damn it!" I said. "I'm trying…"

He makes kind of a snorting laugh and pulls me on. Every time one of these guys has spoken to me I've understood him…except when Paneb spoke that Hittite language. But I can't make anyone understand me. Finally, the big stud stops near the end of the corridor, where there's a big statue…bigger than the others, and facing down the double row. He's got a fancy headdress and costume like a small one in the museum…the one of Osiris. That's the good-guy god, the one that decides if a man goes to heaven or not. And the end idol in the row to his left is just like the big, new one…the one they can't decide if it's Anubis or Seth. Only this one's maybe even bigger than the one Silverman brought back.

Paneb stands me so I'm facing it, and he looks at me as if I'm supposed to say or do something. "Anubis," I say finally.

Paneb laughs like I've really said something funny, and shakes his head. "You need not pretend," he says again. "Seth protects his servants."

Now I really don't know what to do, and I stand there looking at him and looking at the god, and wondering what's going to happen next. This Paneb acts like I'm supposed to be on his side, all right, but I can't talk to him and if I could I don't know what I would'a said. He's holding a metal tool in his hand, the wrench…or key…the thing he used to put the chains on me. He's thinking…wondering if he should turn me loose or not, I figured, and if I could'a said the right thing I guess he would have. Only I can't, and after a little while he sighs and shrugs his shoulders, shoves me back the way we came. He takes me up to where the tunnel forked, and leads me down the other side.

This time, we end up in what's gonna be their version of a jail...a big room with chains bolted into the walls, and stone benches set at different heights along the sides. There's a couple'a guards, but only one other guy who's chained up as a prisoner. Paneb attaches me to the wall, right near this other stud, and then he calls the guard aside and whispers with them for a few minutes. He leaves after that, and the guards come over to look at me.

I'm still chained up with my hands in back of me, and with the irons around my ankles, and now with about ten feet of heavy brass chain attaching me to the wall. The guards are both just kids, small and slender like most of the Egyptians seemed to be. They're laughing together, and looking at my cock. I guess Paneb said something to them about it. The other prisoner is bigger than they are—hairy like me, and just as naked. He's sitting on his bench, but he's free except for the chain around his neck. He's got a big cock resting on the slab between his legs, and I can see he's circumcised. I guess everyone must have been...everyone except me.

One of the guards comes up and fingers my dick, shoving the foreskin back and grinning over his shoulder at the other one. "I wonder if it stays over the head when it's hard," said the guard who was watching.

The one who held my cock shrugged and cupped

his hand around it. "There is one way to find out," he says, and he starts playing with me, sliding his hand along my rod...cool soft fingers holding me while I have to stand there...can't do anything about it, and the kid's making me harder by the minute. Pretty soon it's standing up full, and the kid's fooling with the foreskin, folding it back off the head, then shoving it up so it covers the whole knob.

"Either way," he says to his friend.

Both of 'em are laughing—just kids, like I said, maybe eighteen or nineteen. And the other prisoner, who's probably my age, is sitting there watching it all without saying anything.

"It's big, anyway," says the boy who's playing with me. "Almost as big as Aarak, here." He points to the guy that's chained beside me.

"He's bigger," says the other kid.

They argue, then, laughing back and forth, until the one that was playing with me steps and pulls a small coin out of a pouch at his waist. "Wager?" he says.

The other one agrees, and the guard that's furthest away picks up one of the spears they've left leaning against the other wall. "Come on, Aarak," he says. "Show us!" He prods the other prisoner with the point of his weapon.

The guy looks at him sort of crafty-like. "What may be my reward?" he says. He speaks their language, but he has a different way of pronouncing the words.

The boys whisper together, giggling. "We'll let the biggest one do what he wants to the loser," says one of them, finally.

Aarak grins at 'em and leans back against the wall,

32

starting to play with himself, and I can see right away he's gonna win. He's got a rod on him like…well, I'm not small, but he's hung like a fuckin' bull. It doesn't take him long, and he's got a raging hard-on…must'a been a good inch more than me.

The kids shove us together, facing each other so's our cocks are laid side-by-side, and they can see right away that Aarak's is longer. It's a big, smooth cock with a dark, almost purple head. And his balls are hanging deep and heavy in his sac, with lots of thick black hair all over his groin and up across his belly…onto his chest. He's not very clean, and he has a kind of sour, sweaty smell about him…smudges of dirt on his face and arms.

The kid that bet on me hands his coin to the other and wraps me across the shoulders with the flat of his spear. "You will obey Aarak," he says, and both of 'em step back to watch.

Well, this Aarak stud, he doesn't waste any time. He grabs me around the hips, and he turns me to face my own bench, shoves me down so I'm laying over the edge. There's not much doubt what he wants, and I try to wriggle away from him. He's already just about at the end of his chain, and I wouldn't have to get far to be out of his reach. But the kids both poke me with their spears, and I know better than to try it.

I can hear Aarak spitting on his hands, and then I feel him rubbing thick globs of spit along the crack of my ass. He's got a hard grip on one cheek to hold me still while he rams his fingers up my asshole, greasing it up with saliva. There's nothing I can do, and I can't make them understand me, even if something I might have said would have stopped them. Then I feel the

33

heat of Aarak's hard, hairy thighs against the back of my legs, the shoving of his big cockhead against my ass…and pain, man! Pain, as he shoves that thing into me, and I scream and fall forward on the bench. Then he's all over me, belly against my back, grimy, hairy arms wrapped around my belly and that iron pole shoved up my ass 'til I'm seeing stars it hurts so bad.

I can feel his hot breath against my neck, and his teeth gnawing the flesh at the top of my spine. His hips are driving now, up and down, hard…making that pole fly in and out of me, and his balls are slapping on my thighs. Finally, I collapse against the bench and he keeps fuckin' me like there's no tomorrow, and his breath's coming in short, hard gasps. I'm beginning to get used to it enough so it doesn't hurt so bad, and my own cock's starting to get hard again…just can't help it. 'Course, the kids can see this, and they start laughing and giggling again, making remarks about how much I like it. Then, the one that lost the coin comes up like he's going to whip out his dick and stick it in my mouth. Only about that time Aarak begins to grunt and squeal like a hog in rut, and squeezes his arms about my belly. Deep, heavy groans come out of his mouth and I feel his hot panting against my ear while he shoots his load in me.

When he finishes he stands up, whips his pecker out of my ass and flops back on his own bench. The boys are watching, and I think the one kid is still hot to jab his cock down my throat, only I'm too beat to want it. I pull myself onto the bench, belly down, 'cause otherwise the chains would have cut into my back. I lay there for a while and gradually I start to fall asleep. I hear all three of them talking, but things are starting to get hazy and their words don't make sense, and I don't care anymore. I'm too tired and too sore…aching all over…my feet where I've walked on hot sand and stones, my back and ass—sunburn, I guess…my asshole, my ribs where the soldiers and guards have poked me with their spears.

I fall asleep a few minutes later, and when I do I seem to be falling down a long, black shaft. Down and down, and I want to stop, and I'm thinking if I spread my arms it'll be like wings and I'll float instead of falling. But my wrists are chained so I can't move them…falling, and then I do open my arms and it's all bright blue around me. I'm soaring, flying like a hawk or a gull…gliding without flapping my wings…. And I'm awake, laying on the floor in front of the glass case, and the sunlight's coming in the window.

I sit up after a few minutes, and I figure I've really had a nightmare. Only I'm naked, so I know what I did with Greg was real. Then I try to stand, and my feet hurt like hell! I lean back, and I realize my asshole feels like I've had it from a stallion. I feel my shoulders and upper back, and the skin is hot…red and sunburned, and I've got little scabs along both sides of my rib cage…like I've been bitten by mosquitoes…or pricked with spears.

So, that was the first time, Doc. And I'm not so crazy that I would have believed it, except I had all the marks on me. I hobbled back to my clothes and put them on, standing there in front of that idol. I looked up at his face, and the sunlight is glinting against his ruby eyes. He's looking at me and smiling like he knows. And it's not a Mona Lisa grin anymore. It's a knowing, cocky twist to his face, because he's

Seth. He's the bad-guy god, and he's had me...and he know I know it, and he's laughing at me, Doc! And he's been laughin' at me ever since. He's laughin' at me right now, Doc...right now...

Chapter 4

Tape File No. 686: MASTEN, Gregory K.

Well, I guess you'd say I was sort of a spy, Dr. Lawrence. You see, I graduate from the University this June, and I plan to start off in summer session working for my M.A. There's a dig in Arizona, and I'm already on the list. Only thing is, Dr. Summerfield who's conducting my seminar in Advanced Civilizations, he's also one of the field directors on the dig. Add to that how he's my upper division advisor, and I guess you get the picture.

"I'm not sure I do."

Oh, well...it's just that Dr. Summerfield doesn't agree with Dr. Silverman about the Egyptian collection. He's already published a paper, refuting Silverman's claim to have unearthed a primitive statue of Anubis. He says it's Seth. And if that were true, it would be proof of a theory he's held for a long time that the invaders—the Hyksos—didn't just hold the Delta as far south as Memphis. They ruled Thebes, as well, and extended their domains right to the borders of Nubia—maybe as far as the Fourth Cataract. That would be about Napata, you see.

So, I was supposed to take some measurements off the statue, because Dr. Summerfield had gotten statistics from the Cairo Museum as well as from the Metropolitan in New York. He hoped he could make a convincing argument based on the classic proportions. That's assuming the artists followed the standard ratios and dimensions, which they nearly always did in Egyptian art. That's why I was there, and that's what I was trying to do. Only I wanted to do it so the guard didn't see me. That's why Summerfield didn't come himself. He didn't want to tip Silverman off until he had the proof he needed, and then he'd publish another monograph on it. Publish or perish, you know!

I got to the museum around four in the afternoon, and hour before closing. I saw Ken O'Conner when I first came in, and...he's told you, you say about what we did...so it's no secret. Well, shit, I don't care who knows it! He's a doll, and I dug him...that's all. But I also had to get the professor's measurements. With Ken looking at me the way he was I didn't have much chance of doing it surreptitiously. Then a couple of old ladies came in, and they were more interested in an exhibit of tapestries and wall-hangings in the other room. They kept asking Ken all sorts of questions, and while he was busy I got the statistics off the idol.

Ken didn't stay in the next room any longer than he had to, and he was back with me in about ten minutes.

"We'll be closing in half an hour," he said. "If there's anything special you want to see…I mean, I assume you're a student, so if there's anything I can do to help you…"

"Oh, I'm doing fine," I told him. I looked straight at his basket when I said it, though, and he got the point!

"Stick around," he whispered. "Maybe I can show you some of the more interesting…items—ones we don't have on open display."

"Sound's groovy," I told him.

"It is, baby…it is!" he laughed.

So I stayed until he closed the place, and he was so cocky about the whole thing I figured I'd play it real cool with him. But, I guess he told you about all that. I made him strip and get down on his knees and do me, right in front of the statue. Then, I don't know why, but I just suddenly got the urge to make a real crazy game of it. I had him turn around and I read the inscription on the scroll the idol was holding. No one's been able to translate all of it, by the way, and I wasn't even sure I was getting all the phonetics right. But Ken didn't know the difference, so I just read it through to the end.

I hadn't meant to stay as long as I did, because I was supposed to catch a bus back to the city. But you know, I really grooved on Ken…even if I did give him kind of a hard time—I mean, making him kneel and do me for trade and all. Later, I felt so bad about it I made a point of coming back. Besides, I wanted to look at that idol again. I'd talked to Dr. Summerfield, because that silly grin bothered both of us. He said he wondered if it wasn't the rubies in the eyes that made it seem to smile. The photos—at least the black and white photos—didn't show so profound an expression. Or maybe I just used this as an excuse. Whatever it was I cam back, and I purposely arrived about 4:30.

When he first saw me, Ken's face seemed to light up, and I knew he was glad I'd come. Then, for no reason I could think of, he began to fidget and acted very uncomfortable when I tried to talk to him. "What's wrong?" I asked.

"Nothing," he said.

"Aren't you glad to see me?"

"Oh…oh, sure," he told me. "It's just…just I didn't expect you'd come back."

"Well, I did," I said. "And I'm hoping you'll ask me to stay after school again."

He grinned then, and shrugged. But he still didn't seem to happy.

"If you don't want me, I'll split," I told him.

"No…no, matter of fact I'd really like you to stay." He excused himself, and went to help some tourists who were just coming in.

I sat down on the sarcophagus and really looked the idol over carefully. It didn't matter what angle you stood at, the damned thing still seemed to grin. And I don't think it was just the eyes, although I could see what the professor was talking about. They always seemed to gleam, you see, and that made the whole face kind of twinkle.

Ken showed the other visitors around, and just before five he escorted them to the front door. I heard him lock it behind them. When he came back he was very quiet, almost pensive, and I had to prompt him to get any conversation at all.

"What the hell's the matter?" I asked. "I dig you, man; but if you don't want me here, just say so. I'm not going to…"

"No, I told you it wasn't that," he insisted. "But… well, something funny happened after you left last time. At least, I *think* something funny happened."

He scared me when he said that, because the first thing I could think of was that some object must have been missing. "Jesus, I hope you don't think I took anything!" I said.

"Oh, no!" He finally loosened up, then, and came up to put his arms around me. He kissed me, too, and we…I don't know. That kiss was something a little special, I guess.

"So, tell me what happened," I suggested after we'd sat down. We were right in front of the god, and I wondered if Ken didn't want to go someplace else. I was sure he must have a bunk or bed, someplace where he could sack out over night. But he didn't have any intention of leaving the Egyptian room. He wouldn't tell me what happened, and I think at that point he may have started to have doubts, himself. I mean, I might be thinking I'd dreamed the whole thing, too, except Ken remembers exactly what I do.

"You're certain Ken O'Conner did not relate any of his previous…er…experiences to you, prior to your own?"

I'm completely sure! The first I knew about it was…was when we were in the middle of what happened to both of us.

"All right. Let's go back a moment to your first visit. Did you see or hear…experience anything unusual?"

No…well, nothing I was sure of. I mean, I thought… you know, when I started to come…that gorgeous, hairy

stud kneeling in front of me, all naked and everything...taking my...my...

"Cock. Go ahead, Greg; just speak naturally."

Yeah, he's taking my cock right to the hilt, and I've
got my head tipped back, both hands fastened on his
nape, eyes closed...it seemed...I can't be sure, but I
seemed to be enclosed in some kind of blue fire. I
don't know exactly how to phrase it, but just as I
started to let go the first bolt I was surrounded by this
electric-blue light.

*"Have you ever experienced visual sensations like this
during previous...er, ejaculations?"*

No. This was the only time it ever happened to me.
But still, I was so hot...and it only seemed to last a
couple of seconds. I couldn't be sure, Dr. Lawrence. I
thought I saw it—felt it, but I couldn't be sure. It
might just have been my own responses to what we
did. And if it hadn't been for what happened later, I'd
have let it go at that. Just figured it was one of those
really exceptional moments one experiences in sex. As
it turns out, this first time with Ken was something
that went a little deeper with me, anyway. I mean,
even with the bitchy way I acted that day, I still left
with a feeling...an attachment for him that I hadn't
ever felt for anyone else. Can you understand what
I'm saying, Dr. Lawrence?

"I think so, Greg. You were, or are, in love with Ken?"

I...well, I am now...yes. I don't think I'd put it
quite that strongly for right then. It was just starting...

*"All right. You left that night and you've already
explained how and why you returned. What happened after
that?"*

Well, as I said, Ken was acting a little strangely, and

at first I thought he wasn't too happy about my coming back. But that wasn't it. He didn't tell me what had happened after I'd left, other than to say it was something strange. I tried to question him, and he mumbled something about he guessed he must have fallen asleep and had a nightmare. I don't think he was convinced it was all in his imagination, but he must have been wondering.

We sat in front of the idol for...oh, it must have been half an hour, just talking about nothing, both of us nervous and not quite sure what to say to each other. I already knew I felt...differently...about him, you see, and I guess he felt much the same. Only neither of us was ready to say it. You just don't tell a guy you've only made it with once that you think you're falling in love with him, you know. That's for some silly faggot on the boulevard...someone without the sense to realize that throbbing testicles don't constitute true love.

Finally, though, I couldn't stand it any longer. I put my arms around him and kissed him. He was shaking, almost as if he were afraid. But he responded right away, mouth coming open, drawing my tongue into him, pushing back with his own...holding me so tightly it was almost as if he were clinging to me for...for something more than an exchange of sexual expression. He was still trembling, and even the solid hold we had on one another didn't seem to alleviate it...not for quite a while. Then, he seemed to respond more to me than to whatever it was that troubled him. He began unbuttoning my shirt, and I did the same with him—only it was more complicated to get all that guard uniform off than just the sports shirt and slacks I was wearing.

Finally, without saying anything, both of us stood up and stripped. Ken lighted those lamps at the idol's feet like he did before…must have re-filled them in the meantime, because they gave a brighter, taller flame than I remembered. It was such a wild situation! I mean, almost like a movie set with that grinning idol and the flames, and all the ancient artifacts around us. It's a hard thing to put into words, Dr. Lawrence, and maybe one has to have a feeling for antiquities to appreciate what I'm trying to say. But to me, just the idea of being this close to items that had been made by the hands of men so many thousands of years before…it was exciting, just on its own. Then, with Ken there…naked and ready, and with me feeling the way I did…

"It's my turn," I told him, and I went down on my knees like I'd made him to do me, and I took his cock…already half hard and full, heavy. I pulled it into me and held it, working my tongue all around it as it started to swell harder and harder. His balls had dropped lower, so the sac rested on my chin and his thighs were pressed against my chest like two, warm pillars. He's really hairy, and that turned me on, too! I kept riffling his fur, running my hands all across his belly and reaching up to his chest, pinching his nipples. That seemed to make him all the hotter, because he groaned and rolled his hips, and really started giving me that rod of his.

I brought my hands around behind him, pulling him even harder against me and kept hold of the cheeks of his ass so I could feel the muscles tightening and relaxing. And even relaxed, they were solid! After a while, he reached down and grabbed me under the arms, pulled me back onto my feet. He's a lot shorter than I am, but he's strong as hell...real compact body like he's lifted weights, only I don't think he ever has.

We just stood there, pressed full against one another, kissing and running our hands up and down the other's back while those lamps flickered beside us and all the light from outside gradually faded away. Ken let loose of me...gently freeing himself. "Wait just a minute," he whispered.

I stood by myself in front of the god, watching the flames reflected in his eyes while Ken went into the next room. I guess it was then I had the first feeling of some kind of...of power in that carving. It was as if that ancient god were transmitting some kind of force. I don't know. It's nothing I can put my finger on, only that the black stone face seemed animated, and the power he'd been granted by his ancient creators was somehow there...drawing me to him. I remember thinking if I touched its surface I'd feel the warmth of life, not just cold stone, like something that's been dead and gone since before the start of time. I was about to reach out for it when Ken came back.

"Hope no one catches me doing this," he said. "This is a prize example of Oriental craftsmanship." He was carrying a heavy prayer rug...a Persian carpet about six or seven feet long. It was mostly reds and blues, woven into a typically intricate, medallion pattern. "This isn't on display, yet," he added laughing. "As long as we don't get pecker tracks all over it, I guess what they don't know won't hurt them."

I still wasn't sure just why he wanted to stay there instead of going into the back, but by then I didn't care. Not only because I was so hot and ready that it didn't make any difference, but there was this...thing with the idol, like I told you. I had the feeling we were doing something—how can I tell you? We were doing something not exactly wrong, but it was as if we were going to perform on a stage in front of an audience. What we did together wasn't wrong, in and of itself. I've never felt that having sex with another guy was bad or evil. That wasn't the point. But just like the Danish sex clubs, or the topless joints...what these people actually do isn't wrong or bad. I don't think it's anybody's business to tell them they can't do it in front of others as long as everyone is acting under his own power, so to speak. Yet, there is a certain carry-over from all the things we've been taught as children. To engage in sex—of any kind—this is an act of questionable propriety under any circumstances but the ones in the big book. To do it in front of someone else...well, you know what I'm talking about, Dr. Lawrence. And to me, it seemed as if the ancient gods of Egypt were watching everything we did...watching and laughing at us.

Ken spread his rug on the floor, between the idol and the sarcophagus. We were both lying on it a moment later, tangled arms and legs, and lips pressed together, and hard cocks shoved one against the other until it didn't make a damn who was watching us— whether the whole scene was naughty-naughty or not. I forgot about the god and about where we were, and everything else. All I was aware of was Ken's hot, groovy body against me, and his hands and his lips, and his big hard cock between my thighs.

I had a pretty good idea what he wanted this round, because when he'd come back with the rug I'd seen him stick a tube of K-Y underneath his clothes. He did it covertly, as if it was a guilty thought, which sort of turned me on all the more. But he didn't seem in any hurry to use it. After we'd been there quite a while, he swung himself around so we could each take the other's cock. And we stayed that way for a long time. I never was really gone on the sixty-nine bit, but with Ken it was something else! Holding his cock in my mouth, and feeling him working on mine...sliding his lips along the shaft and driving the cockhead down his throat while I was doing the same to him.... It was almost like being able to feel both sides of it...doing it and having it done to you all at once.

Then I was coming, and the boiling, burning juice was setting my nuts on fire! I couldn't sink it deep enough or crush myself down hard enough against him. My eyes were closed, and I felt the waves of fantastic release, and I knew I was shooting everything I had into him...and as I came there was that blue light again. But I was so completely embroiled in fucking Ken I couldn't pay any attention to anything else. It just seemed the lights were flashing inside of me while I poured it all into the heat and moisture...

I opened my eyes, because where my arms had gone under Ken's chest, and where I'd felt the rug against my skin there was suddenly a cold, hard surface. The final spasms were racking my body, but I lifted myself up a bit...and when I raised my head I could see we weren't in the museum anymore! The idol was still in front of us, still grinning like it always had. But there was a long line of other gods beside it, and to our left was Osiris—bigger than all the others.

The chamber was lighted by a pair of torches set

along the wall behind the largest god, with shadows growing heavier toward the distant end. "What the hell... Where are we?" I gasped.

"That's what I was afraid to tell you," said Ken. "I don't know, but it's like what happened to me before."

Chapter 5

Tape File No. 686: MASTEN, Gregory K. (Con't)

I was so stunned by what had happened...or what appeared to have happened, I just hung there, both hands pressed against the stones, chest raised, my cock still in Ken's ass, but growing softer by the second. It was like nothing I had ever seen, or even dreamed of. We were in a long hall, obviously below ground, with a row of stone gods along the wall in front of us, and a facing row along the opposite side. To our left, gazing down the double ranks of idols was the largest of them all, a great huge statue of Osiris, carved out of dark, green granite.

Moving as if in a dream, or a trance, I slipped free of Ken and stood up. We were both stark naked, of course, which made it seem all the more as if I must have been dreaming.

"Do you often have dreams where you are nude?"

No, not often. But I have had a couple like that, and I certainly wouldn't be running around without clothes unless it was a dream!

"Well," I said, "I don't know where we are, but at least our old friend Anubis came with us."

"It's not Anubis," said Ken flatly. "It's Seth."

I looked at him in surprise, because I couldn't imagine his knowing this, at least not knowing it and sounding so certain about it. "I don't get it," I said. "I thought..."

"They told me," he said.

"They? Who are they?"

And that's when Ken explained how it had happened to him before. He almost cried, because he said he hadn't meant to get me into it. But after a couple of days he'd convinced himself it must all have been his imagination. "We really are here, though, aren't we?" he asked.

"I guess we are," I said.

"But how...?"

I shrugged. "You got me, baby," I told him. I started off, down the row of idols, looking at each one and trying to figure out just what kind of place we were in. I thought at first it might be the basement of the museum...that we'd fallen through a trap door of some kind. But Ken assured me that wasn't it.

So, I examined each idol in turn. Next to Anubis—or Seth—was Troth, the god with the baboon head, who was supposed to be the keeper of wisdom. Next to him was Sobek, the crocodile god of water, worshipped much further north, and generally thought of as belonging to Heliopolis. Between him and Osiris was Isis...the sister-goddess of the Nile. I trotted on, further down the row, my bare feet making a whispering sound against the stones, and even this subtle noise echoed along the empty vault.

I cannot tell you how strange and helpless I felt, a single, naked mortal surrounded by the huge stone effigies of the mighty Egyptian gods. The air was dry and warm against my skin, and other than a slight mustiness there was an almost total absence of any sensory stimuli. I could see the gods, of course, but they were silent, placid in their unmoving grandeur. There was no sound whatever, and even the temperature was benign, neither warm nor cold, and the air about me was as still as the ranks of silent deities.

Near the end, the hall became so dark I could not make out the features on the farthest idols. Had I climbed up on them, and peered into their faces I might have discerned their identities. But to touch them would have required more courage than I possessed. Instead, I started back toward Ken. He stood watching me, rooted to the spot where I had left him, as if afraid we might somehow become separated if he moved.

My thought was to take one of the torches that guttered on the wall behind Osiris, and use it to light my way into the dark end of the hall. Until that moment, I had not considered the possibility of another person being anywhere near us. It was as if the stillness of the hall proclaimed its being the domain of just the gods—totally beyond the reach of mortal man. But the presence of the torches was certain evidence of some human instrumentality, and I suddenly felt the creeping fingers of fear about my heart.

I took Ken's hand when I reached him, and together we approached the great statue of Osiris. We stood gazing up at the serene features on this father of the gods, neither of us willing to commit the sacrilege of climbing over his stony facade to reach the torches that blazed to either side of his head. Unless we did climb on him, though, there was no way we were going to get to them. Even if one of us stood on the other's shoulders, we would not be able to reach. That is how huge these statues were, Dr. Lawrence. The one of Osiris must have been at least twenty-five feet tall.

We were standing there, neither of us knowing just what to suggest, when a portion of the wall in back of the god slid open, and a reddish glow of light filtered into the chamber. A tall, slender old man in the very ornate, ceremonial robes of a High Priest came toward us. He was followed by a line of eight or nine completely shaved, completely naked young men. All of them were chanting some sort of cadence, and they moved with a stiff, almost mechanical precision.

We saw them before they saw us—not that it did us any good, because there wasn't any place to run. "That Nebnofer," whispered Ken. "He's the…"

The chanting ended abruptly, as Nebnofer stared at us in disbelief. "The outer door is locked," he said.

As Ken had told me happened to him, I was able to understand the priest's words. I think he spoke a variety of the ancient dialects I had studied in school, as I seemed to recognize the accented syllables. However, my perception involved more than the words themselves. Hearing a language spoken is much different from sounding out phonetics expressed by the drawings in a row of hieroglyphics.

The High Priest continued to stare at us, while his naked followers crowded behind him, not unlike a flock of chicks huddling behind their mother for protection. Indecision was plain on the old man's features, though he seemed awed by our presence...awed, and maybe a little afraid. "How did you come here?" he asked at length.

"You know some of the lingo," whispered Ken. "See if you can make him understand we aren't spies." With this, my friend moved slightly behind me, and from the corner of my eye I saw that he was pushing back his foreskin. "This is what got me in trouble the last time," he muttered.

"We are come...from a distant land," I managed to say. "We are..." I didn't know the word for "friends," and could only think of *nefer*, which means "beautiful," though in Dr. Summerfield's interpretation it implies more of the Spanish *simpatico* than just physical attractiveness.

Whatever I actually expressed, Nebnofer responded with a slow, sage nodding of his head. "You must truly be children of the gods," he said. "Else you could never have entered the sacred chamber." I seemed almost as if the power which permitted me to understand his spoken words was allowing me to sense the very fringe of his emotional projection as well, because there was still a note of suspicion behind the graciousness of what he actually said. This should have been a warning to us, but again there was little we could have done, regardless.

I tried to think, but I'm afraid my mind was boggled by everything that had happened. I still struggled against a basic urge to disbelieve what was passing before my eyes. I wanted to say something more, yet couldn't frame any reasonable thought into the limited range of my vocabulary. As a result, we just stood staring at them, and they at us. Then one of the young men behind the High Priest stood on tip-toe and whispered something into the old man's ear. Nebnofer smiled, and gestured for us to stand aside. It was a gentle motion, and implied an element of grudging respect.

"We must complete our rite," he explained apologetically. "The acolytes must dedicate themselves to Osiris before the orb of Re returns."

Pulling Ken with me, I stepped out of their way, and the procession—less perfectly in line, now, and with the boys obviously more interested in us than they were in completing their ritual—filed past. First, they grouped themselves in front of Osiris, the High Priest in the middle, and the others ranged in a semicircle behind him. They bowed and went through a stiffly formal obeisance...asking the greater god's permission, as best I could understand it, before proceeding down the line of stone figures.

They next stopped in front of Troth—the god with the head of a baboon. They prayed to him, asking that he grant them the knowledge to serve. "He's the moon god," I whispered to Ken. "It must be night, and I'd guess it's a full moon."

"As long as they don't all turn into werewolves," he mumbled grimly.

I laughed, in spite of my own fears. "That's the wrong culture...wrong century," I assured him.

"Well, I'm glad you find it so educational," replied my companion. "Now that you've seen it, and now that I've proved I'm not the only freak, why don't you figure how to get us the fuck outta here?"

When they finished their little session before the moon-god, they started back, making a short prayer to Anubis—or Seth—as they passed. It was a peculiar ritual, and as I listened to them I was reminded of some church prayer, where one asks a saint to intercede with God. Only here, they were praying that Anubis grant them favor in the eyes of his master. That would be Osiris.

"They obviously don't agree with you," I said to Ken. "They're calling him Anubis."

"They should know," he replied. "Only Paneb… that's the one who chained me up last time…Paneb says it's Seth, and he seemed to think it was funny as all shit…"

"If the children of the god will honor us," said Nebnofer, pausing in front of us, "we would like to make them comfortable."

"I'm hungry," whispered Ken. "Maybe we'll get a good meal out of it."

We followed the High Priest, and the flock of young acolytes clustered behind us. I didn't have the feeling we were prisoners, though I'm sure they would have stopped us if we had tried to get away. No one spoke again until we had passed through the doorway behind the idol of Osiris. The stone slab ground shut, after amends for whatever previous…misunderstanding there may have been."

The old priest conducted us to a wide chamber off the main hall.

Two of the boys brought a wide, low table, which they placed before our couches, positioned so each of us could reach it. Then a couple of others brought ewers and goblets, offering us large servings of an amber-colored wine. Very quickly, the table was loaded with an assortment of dried figs and plums, fresh grapes and a dish of some fruit that looked like apples, but with more of an orange-yellow color. There were sesame cakes covered with thick honey syrup, several kinds of nut-meats, and a platter of tiny roasted birds.

We both drank deeply of the wine, and Ken was soon munching away on something that looked a little like popcorn. The boys kept bringing it to him in quantities, once they saw he particularly liked it. Nebnofer joined us after a few minutes, and I moved over to allow him room on my couch. He seemed to accept this as a token of divine favor, and sat down with evident pleasure. He nodded at Ken, who was still tossing down handfuls of his unknown delicacy.

"What is that?" I managed to ask.

"Oh, it is my favorite, too," said the High Priest. He reached across me and picked up several of the small, crisp puffs. He popped a couple into my mouth, then a few into his own. "Locusts," he explained. "Fried in the finest fat and shelled by maidens in the Temple of Isis."

Since I'll eat about anything, the idea of devouring French-fried grasshoppers didn't bother me; but Ken turned green. I saw him looking about in desperation for a place to spit the mouthful he'd been chewing when Nebnofer spoke.

"Swallow it, baby," I told him. "Otherwise you'll offend the gods. Besides, you've had worse!"

Nebnofer was still sitting next to me, and as we

spoke I could see puzzlement wrinkle his brow. All around us, the boys were joking together, a couple of them wrestling and others feeding themselves or their companions. Three young men had slipped into the room from the farther end. They began to play a weird, tinkling melody on a collection of ancient instruments. One had a tall lute that sounded much like a Japanese koto. Another had a smaller, harp-like lyre, while the third played a hollow, reedy flute.

"I must admit...to be perfectly honest," confessed the High Pries, "I do not know if you are truly children of the gods, or whether you may be innocent travelers as you claim. I know the ways of the gods are strange, and I know you..." he inclined his head toward Ken, "...were mistreated by Paneb several days ago. He was furious because you escaped his jailers."

"Paneb is not your...your..." Again I fumbled for a word meaning "friend."

Nebnofer shook his head. "Paneb enjoys the favor of Pharaoh," he said solemnly, "but we fear..." his hand moved in an arc that encompassed the entire group, "...we suspect he may be in league with Sethos."

"I don't get it," muttered Ken.

Nebnofer looked at us curiously. Quickly, I tried to explain the situation to Ken as best I could understand it. "If I've guessed right," I told him, "and assuming this isn't just one, big nightmare...we've somehow gotten ourselves into Egypt during the Seventeenth Dynasty. That's what historians call the Time of Troubles, when the Kingdom of Memphis had fallen to Semitic invaders—Syrians and the ancestors of what probably became the Hebrew tribes. The Egyptians called these people Hyksos, or desert people. Their kinds took the title of Pharaoh and tried to extend their power through both Upper and Lower Egypt. According to history they never made it, and the rulers of Thebes finally drove them out…but not for another hundred years."

"In other words, we're in the middle of a civil war," suggested Ken.

"Something like that," I said, "except the books don't record the Hyksos getting this far south. If we're in the area that later became Abu Simbel, then we're between the first and second cataract, near the city of Sebua…"

"Sebua?" said Nebnofer. "Yes, Pharaoh is in Sebua."

"See?" I said. "It's beginning to make some sense."

"But what about the gods and this Sethos character?"

"My guess is, both sides have spies," I said, "and this Sethos must be the opposition's James Bond. Whatever he's trying to pull off, it involves that grinning idol—Seth or Anubis, whichever it turns out to be."

"And these Hyksos, they worshipped Sethos?" asked Ken.

"Well, not Sethos," I laughed. "Sethos seems to be the chief spy…magician as they call him. Seth is the god, and this man would be his 'servant.'"

"And Paneb?"

I shrugged.

"I cannot understand your speech," said Nebnofer softly, "but I hear you mention the names of the gods. May I ask…whom you serve, and what you do here?"

I looked at him helplessly, spreading my hands in the universal gesture of indecision. Even if I could have spoken his language, how do you explain to a bronze-age priest that you've somehow traveled three millennia and half-way around a world he doesn't even know exists beyond his horizons? Christ, I can't even explain it to you, doctor! Neither of us said any more until Ken broke the silent impasse.

He was beginning to feel his wine, I guess, because he started to laugh, giggle really. "Ask him to take you to his leader," he suggested.

"Unfortunately," I replied, "He is the leader, or damned near it."

Now, Dr. Lawrence, I know I'm admitting I took this seriously, and I know I'm making myself sound more deluded and crazy by telling you about it. But to me...at the time...it was all very real. I decided Nebnofer must have been a priest of Osiris. This meant he worshipped the entire hierarchy of Theben gods, including Re, who had apparently not become as powerful as he would later on. I also remembered all the movies and stories about appeasing the witch-doctor, and saving your ass by not threatening him. So, in my broken Egyptian, I told him we were servants of Anubis. This made us followers of a lesser god, you see, and claiming this we made no pretense to a power greater than his.

It seemed to work, because Nebnofer patted my knee and personally refilled my goblet. He sat drinking with me for a long time, while the shaved, naked boys cavorted about us and the musicians played their clinking, increasingly lively tunes in the background. For the moment, at least, we were safe from Paneb, who did seem to be the villain of the whole piece.

I guess the boys had been holding back a little up to now, because when I finished speaking with the High Priest, he said something to them about our being "truly honored guest." Almost immediately after that, we had them swarming all over us. Several of the lamps had burned down, and no one bothered to refill them. The room was darker than it had been before, but it was comfortably warm and there was an odor of incense in the air. Except for Nebnofer and the three musicians, everyone was as naked as before...Ken and myself, as well as the troop of boys. The wine was deceptively mellow, and before I realized it I was more than a little drunk.

Both Ken and I had been eating the various foods, some of which were sticky—mostly with natural honey and the syrup that forms on dried fruits. The boys brought bowls of scented water and bathed our hands and faces, then continued to give us a more thorough going-over. Ken was especially intriguing to them, because of that damned foreskin. Circumcision was performed on all males at birth, I guess, both in Egypt and in the lands of the Hyksos. Even today, both Arabs and Jews do it, as you know, the custom stems from long before. The only people of that period who didn't do it were the Hittites—Egypt's arch enemies from what is now Turkey—and I think the Babylonians. During this particular period there must not have been much trade with an outside area, so I guess none of the boys had ever seen a natural cock before.

But Ken wasn't getting all the attention by any means. As I lay back, sipping the sweet, amber wine, I felt what seemed like dozens of hands laving my body with warm, moist towels. Through half-closed eyes I could see the boys working on Ken, who responded almost immediately—and obviously—to their treatment. Of course, I could feel my own energies rebuilding, and I wasn't very far behind him. Because we'd been...transported at the height of our sex, I'm sure Ken hadn't come. So if there was a whore in the crowd it was me! In just a few minutes I had a raging hard-on, and this attracted some very decided interest from the youngsters. I was also a curiosity to them, you see, because I'm blond and fair-skinned, much lighter than any Egyptian. I'm also a little over six feet, which made me a giant by their standards, and my cock... well, my cock is proportionate to the rest of me.

At some point, Nebnofer withdrew. I had my eyes closed, just enjoying what was happening to me, so I didn't see him leave. I just know he was beside me one minute, and when I looked again he was gone. It didn't seem to make any difference; by then the boys were keeping me more than entertained. This was their equivalent of a graduation party, I supposed, with Ken and myself forming their special, unexpected treat.

Our couches were covered with a soft, smooth leather that felt almost like human skin. It must have been impervious to most fluids...either that or the boys were unconcerned about damaging them, because after bathing us they began oiling our bodies. What they used was a viscous substance, like olive oil, heavily perfumed with a spicy, bitter-sweet fragrance. Warm, gentle hands began rubbing this into my skin, layer after layer, covering every inch of my body as they eased me from back to belly, and over again. I could see that the youngsters were taking turns, working in shifts, some on me and others on Ken...then changing off. At all times, though, I was surrounded by gleaming, slender bodies, dark skins reflecting the ruddy glow of guttering lamps. One of the boys was kneeling beside me on the couch, his hands stroking my upper chest and shoulders, his tight little belly arched across me and his well-formed cock dangling a tantalizing few inches above my hand.

Moving slowly, because in truth I was so intoxicated the whole scene was more like a dream than anything else, I slipped one arm around the kid's waist and grasped the nape of his neck with the other. I drew him down against me, until his slick, oil-coated chest slid on mine. I kissed him, gently at first, and then with greater force, driving his lips apart with my tongue and probing deep into the sweetness of his mouth. This surprised him, I think, as such total exchange may not have been common among them. He responded almost immediately, however, sliding his arms about me, while his friends chattered in gleeful pleasure behind him.

But the arts of physical love were not totally lacking among them, and while they may not have known to kiss as we do, they certainly were expert in other modes of expression. The boy I held against me was curled across my chest, so his loins were pressed to my hips, leaving my midsection and groin exposed. In moments, I felt cloying fingers lift my cock and balls, stroking softly along the risen shaft and hefting the balls, as if to test their weight. Then the moist warmth of lips encircled the crown, while at the same instant another mouth absorbed my nuts, drawing them in with an easy, sucking motion while the first descended along the shaft of my penis.

I could not see them, but the two who possessed me were curled against my legs and groin, while the boy whose lips joined with mine began a slow, sliding rhythm against my side. I could feel his hard little cock traveling across my skin and I tightened my grip about his body. Other hands were stroking me, and it seemed I was touched by a multitude of seeking fingers and caressing palms. I now encircled two young bodies in my arms, while the two who worked upon my cock and balls continued as they had before. Yet another was easing my thighs apart, stroking the inner curves of my ass.

Where I was and how I got there no longer mattered to me. I was blanketed in warm, living flesh...youth-hard bodies and willing, eager beauty. The coating of oil made the sensuous contacts extremely arousing, yet somehow more subtle and...I guess I'd call it "unified." When I closed my eyes it was as if a single entity enclosed me; the pressure against my torso, lips, midsection—all were like one. The dimly lighted chamber spun like a slowly accelerating merry-go-round, and the loving, tender movements drove me into such a state of euphoric arousal I was...I felt like I had once when some friends talked me into trying grass. Actually, I think there may have been something in the wine, because I felt a tingle—a tickle almost—pumping through my balls and all along the urethra.

I was getting dangerously close, so I wriggled free of the kid who was working on my cock. The other, the one who'd been sucking my nuts, had left off by then, and was tonguing the insides of my thighs. When I moved, my new position allowed me to catch another glimpse of Ken. I have to admit that for a minute I wasn't completely happy about it. I guess it was the realization I'd really fallen for the guy, because seeing him belly-down on top of a tall, slender boy, fucking the kid like there was no tomorrow, I felt a twinge of jealousy! Buried as I was in my own pile of sucking, loving boys…but love isn't supposed to be logical, especially when you've had more than you should to drink.

The irrational moment passed, and I was again involved with my personal vagaries. While Ken's behavior was not forgotten, the sensuous rise and fall of his ass, the flexing sinews beneath oiled and gleaming skin became a source of arousal rather than displeasure. His example was a good one, I decided, and I began taking stock of those who lay with me, wondering which boy would make the best object for a similar impalement.

I chose a delicate, slender lad, whose shaven head would barely have grazed my throat had we stood facing one another. His arms and chest were sleek and smooth, with an attractive, symmetrical outline of muscular development. While his shoulders were fairly broad for his height, his tiny waist could almost be spanned by the combined width of my hands. His little ass was round…perfect! It reflected a ruddy glow in the feeble light, and I thought of the poem where they called it a "rosy-cheeked beacon."

Amidst expressions of amusement from his companions, I made it clear I wanted him to lie beside me, and after this the other boys moved away. A couple of them seemed disappointed, which was flattering, I guess…but I soon forgot about them. I pulled the beautiful, unresisting kid against me, then slid myself on top of him. I felt his cock snap across mine as I aligned our bodies and shoved my mouth hard against his. Sensuously, his flesh moved in reciprocation to my mounting demands, until I maneuvered my iron between his thighs. He clamped against it, which created a firm, kind of possessing channel.

As a partner, he was outta sight! He seemed to merge with me, and his body fitted so comfortably with mine it almost seemed as if he conformed to my specific requirements…like we were *supposed* to meet and join, despite the miles and the centuries that had separated us. His mouth was sweet and warm and it didn't take him any time to acquire the art of kissing like a Westerner.

I still felt an occasional hand or sometimes an entire body brush across the oil-slick surface of my back. But these grew less as my concentration focused on the boy I'd selected. I held him prostrate, crushed between me and the leather-covered couch. I paid little attention to anyone else, now, though I was vaguely aware that several of our companions had paired off and were emulating us on the floor or the nearby benches.

By the time I finally raised myself and turned my young man onto his belly, only a couple of lamps were still burning. The dry, warm air had taken on a subtle fragrance and a cloying moisture from the bodies that twisted and acted out their rites of love around us. Both my companion and myself were sweating, our bodies seeming to melt into one another while a furnace heat surrounded us. My hardened cock had once again slipped between his thighs; only this time its gentle, plunging motion carried it near and past the desired opening. Finally, on one particularly high-risen, upward stroke. I felt my cockhead slip higher between his cheeks. Its tip brushed across the hidden recess, hanging there a moment until I pressed down, driving it toward the proper point. Volitionally unguided by his hand or mine, it penetrated the channel as I resettled my loins against the rounded curves of his ass.

Beneath me, my lithe, responding partner groaned deeply, acknowledging the demand of rigid flesh. For only a moment the muscular ring resisted me. Then, as if in answer to some deep, unspoken invitation, my cock sunk into the tight-stretched flesh. The waves of sensation rose like wisps of steamy bliss. It surrounded me and drove me into an oblivion…. [Long pause, followed by the patient's laughter.] I guess I got a little carried away, Dr. Lawrence. But he was a beautiful kid, even with every hair shaved off his body. He was delicate, but masculine—in that stage between being a boy and a man. Fucking him, with our bodies all slippery with oil…I've never felt anything like it!

Looking across, I could see Ken getting close to the end. His ass would draw tight, raise a bit, and slam down hard against the kid. The boy's legs were spread so wide apart, he'd actually hooked his knees around the edges of the couch. And Ken was giving it to him without any pause or holding back! Watching made me all the hotter, if that was possible. I started shoving my cock in and out, faster and harder, until I forced a rattling groan from the boy every time I connected with him. The way the cheeks of his ass fit up against me excited a feeling almost as intense as from the pressure of his muscle-ring about my dick.

I saw Ken slam one home, then arch his body, straining so he was all hard muscle and tight-stretched skin. I knew he was shooting his load, and though I hadn't been quite ready myself, that was all she wrote! Seeing him sent me spinning into that blind moment when you don't see or hear or know anything except the roar of your own blood in your ears and the fantastic surge of boiling jit—shooting up from between your legs, making your balls pull tight, and then the blast of sensation down your cock! I shoved myself all the way into the nameless kid beneath me, and felt him rear up against my loins while I hung on his back and gave him everything I had! And by then it was quite a bit.

After a long time, my body settled back to normal and I began to notice other items and people around me. We were down to one oil lamp; and that wasn't very bright. My boy had gotten up and was hunting for a towel to sponge me off. Ken was sitting on the edge of his couch.

"Man, what I wouldn't give for a cigarette, right now," he laughed. "Don't suppose you got one hidden...someplace, have you?"

"Just a big, limp cigar," I told him.

He came over and sat beside me while one of the boys brought us more wine. Because sex had made us thirsty, we both drank more than we should of it. Ken laid down beside me, and I closed my eyes. I don't know where the boys had gone...the boys we'd been with, I mean. There were several stretched out on the grass mats a few feet away from us, but I think my kid had gone over to the couch where Ken had been. Those last swigs of wine just about did me in. The room was spinning again, and it occurred to me that Nebnofer might have slipped us something. Probably not...probably just that we'd drunk too much.

Anyway, Ken was asleep, curled against me. My arm was around him, his head resting against my shoulder when I dozed off. The last I recall was the final lamp starting to sputter and go out, but I was gone before the room became completely dark. I remember a lyre playing in the background, but the other musicians had given up...joining the temple boys, I think, but even that I wasn't sure about...

The next I knew I was blinking against strong sunlight. Ken was still in my arms, but we were lying on the Persian rug in front of the idol...and it was morning. When I tried to sit up I awakened Ken. He stared blindly for a couple of seconds, then jumped to his feet and started hunting for his watch. "Seven-thirty," he said. "We've got about half an hour."

Chapter 6

Masten had gone on to describe their rush to get dressed and replace the rug before Sam, the other guard, arrived. Greg had slipped out the back way, which ended his account except for the expressions of confused logic by which he tried to explain what had happened. The tape ran out while he was in the middle of this, but Dr. Lawrence had taken notes. It was all too clear the young man believed the reality of what he related, and that was enough to justify retaining him. The police had reported the confinement to his family, of course, and though his parents were upset, they lived in another state and had thus far not put in an appearance. Because of the burglary charge, a court order had been issued for his continued diagnostic treatment—despite the fact that Silverman, the owner of the museum, had apparently not yet signed a complaint.

O'Conner was another situation, Dr. Lawrence realized. He was not involved with the police, and unless there was more justification, he would be released in another day or two. Regardless how bizarre O'Conner's fantasies, he was not a menace to society.

Paul Lawrence returned his tapes to their proper files, ready to stretch out on the cot that served both as "couch" and his home-away-from-home. It was already late, and he was on call for eight in the morning. He might as well stay over, and try to reach a decision. He had to consider both the welfare and the rights of these two men—this pair of human beings. If he held the one, he should somehow find an excuse to keep the other. Either that, or let both of them go and try to forget the whole thing. In a way, he wished he could. But the old maxim about unsolved puzzles held true for him as any patient. *The problems we solve may afterward be forgotten; those that remain unanswered... those which do not allow us to attain closure, these stay with us, plague us and taunt our memories.*

In the darkened office, the doctor slipped off his shirt and pants, hanging them carefully in the small closet. Shoes and socks were already on the floor beneath his desk, shirt draped across the corner. He dropped on the cot and unfolded a blanket to cover his feet and lower legs. It was too warm for more. Lying in just his shorts, recalling the accounts of his patients, he felt the greater warmth about his loins and an incontestable, adolescent urge. His cock swelled into his hand, finding its own freedom through the parted front of his boxer shorts. *Big and hard, big as Masten, maybe...shouldn't...it's what my patients do in their isolated cells...laughed at by attendants. Well, no attendants*

*around to see…no one to know or care…and that's the thing,
isn't it…no one to know.*

"Oh, excuse me, Doctor Lawrence!" Miss Gleason
backed, red-faced out the door, pulling it shut gently
behind her.

Paul Lawrence smiled, stretching and coming full
awake in the space of a single heart-beat. He looked
down at himself, grinning…firm chest and midsection,
not as tanned as he might be, but ruddy and healthy
looking. He still wore his shorts, but it wouldn't have
mattered. The lower portion of his body was
concealed by the blanket…*old prude! Shit, she should
have seen enough naked men by this time…been a nurse since
the Year One! All a matter of status…like they told me when
I faced the Board of Medical Examiners…pretend they're
all sitting in front of you in their underdrawers…makes it
easier…*

Moving no faster than he must, he shuffled across
to the closet for a terry-cloth robe. Dressed in this, and
carrying his ditty-bag, he shoved the door open and
padded down the hall to the interns' shower room.
Miss Gleason forced a smile as he passed her desk,
and he returned it in kind.

He found an unoccupied shower stall, and felt his
mood brightening as the warm needle spray cascaded
against his body. Rivers of soapy water across the
chest, running together on his belly, down the groin
and through the pubic hair…*falling off my cock like a
horse taking a piss…remember once when Dad took us to
that farm for the summer? That fuckin' thing was a gelding,
too…*

He dried himself in the area adjoining the showers.

Rows of lockers lined the opposite wall, and several young men were changing clothes...arriving or going off shift. *Some of those new interns...one over there looks like the young number on that TV show. Doctor dramas are getting popular again, I guess. With talent like that...talk about horses! And that's no gelding...balls like.... Stop it! Be springing a rod right here in the shower room, and how would that look? ITEM IN HOSPITAL BULLETIN: Horny psychiatrist goes berserk! Rapes innocent young intern...*

"Hi, Paul! Stay over last night?" It was Eddie Gold, "his" intern.

"Got hung up on a case, and stayed so late.... Say, aren't you on days again?" The young man was stripping, obviously getting ready to shower.

"Yeah, but I didn't get home last night either...play, not work!" He laughed, turning away as he slipped off his shorts. Quickly wrapping a towel around his waist he covered the couple of yards to the shower.

Wonder what he's got? Either too much or not enough, probably. Jewish, so he's gotta be circumcised, but most of us are...except O'Conner. Here we go again. Never realized Gold had such a good build, though...not just wiry, but firm and round and fully packed...how'd it go? Cigarettes... cancer-sticks. But what I'd give for one right now! Just a phallic symbol, Paul...just...

Still dressed in his robe, he re-entered Miss Gleason's outer office. "Your coffee and roll are on your desk, doctor," said the nurse. "And Mr. Silverman is sitting beside it," she added smugly.

"Thanks," he said. *Old battle-axe! Silverman's here. Hum, interesting! From Lady Gleason's attitude, he must have blood in his eyes.* "Mr. ...er, Dr. Silverman," he said brightly, extending his hand. "Hope you'll excuse my attire, but things were a little hectic yesterday, and I spent the night."

"It's a pleasure to meet you, Dr. Lawrence," Silverman replied evenly. He had lifted his butt a couple of inches off the chair when he shook hands, and now settled down again.

"I understand your an anthropologist," remarked Dr. Lawrence. "Uh, care for a cup of coffee?"

"Yes, on both counts," Silverman seemed to discard some of his reserve, then, to replace it with an almost professional charm. A man in his early thirties, Walter Silverman was lean and handsome, in a dark Semitic way. His sharp features were even and well formed, with a long, rather slender nose above full, sensuous lips. His thick, curly, black hair formed a gray-edged widow's peak above his brow. He was dressed in an obviously expensive olive blazer, with grey-green slacks and buff-brown Italian shoes. His easy confidence bore subtle testimony to his wealth, while his flowing, articulate speech clearly evidenced an extensive education.

"I presume you're here about O'Conner," said Dr. Lawrence. Feeling a bit self-conscious, he proceeded to hang his robe in the closet. Standing naked, sideways to the other man, he unfolded a clean pair of shorts. Silverman was watching him, but his interest seemed casual, in keeping with his overall demeanor. "I hope you'll forgive me," added the doctor, "but I've got to…"

"Think nothing of it," replied Silverman. "Yes, I am curious about O'Conner, and I'm anxious to find out just what you think of this story he's telling."

"Have you seen him?"

"Yes."

"Then, I take it he told you about this...this fantasy of his?"

Silverman nodded, grey eyes gazing solemnly at the psychiatrist, who was now buttoning his shirt, and had yet to don his trousers. "What I'd like to know is how you feel about it."

"How should I feel?" replied Paul Lawrence defensively. He pulled on his pants and stuffed his shirt inside them. As he buckled his belt, Silverman pulled out a pack of cigarettes and offered them to him. With the greatest of self-control, Dr. Lawrence waved them off. "No thank you."

"I gather you don't buy it, then?" The anthropologist's tone was more a statement than a question, but his upper lip curled in just the faintest trace of a grin.

"O'Conner's story? How can I believe it?"

"I guess each of us would qualify as a scientist," said Silverman, "but we face the traditional dilemma of any professional who is confronted by a metaphysical problem. We don't want to accept it, yet we can't see any other explanation."

"Are you telling me you can buy this...teleportation—time travel—however you'd name what these boys are telling us?"

Silverman smiled at his companion, a twisted grin that hung somewhere between being ironic and grim. "What I'm saying..." he began. Then he exhaled sharply, making a whistling sound through his nostrils. "Did you ever read much detective fiction?" he asked abruptly. "I mean the classic writers...Agatha Christie back to Conan Doyle...Ellery Queen, Nero Wolfe...the standards?"

"Well, when I was a kid I guess I read most of them," said Dr. Lawrence with a shrug, "...about as the average person, I'd say."

"Well, in my younger days I went through all of these like a hot knife through butter. I got so I could usually pick the murderer after the first clue had fallen, or just feel him out because I knew the writer's style. I read Sherlock Holmes from start to finish, and while Doyle made a lot of boo-boos—made Holmes deduce solutions when he hadn't eliminated all the alternatives—he did have a favorite maxim that always stuck with me: *Eliminate the impossible. Whatever remains, however, improbable, must be the truth.* Now, Holmes didn't always stick to this in his own deductions, but the basic rule is nonetheless valid."

"Isn't that what we're doing when we reject the idea of two men being transported through time and space...from the twentieth century to...to what? The Seventeenth Dynasty, I think was Masten's estimate. I'd be inclined to reject that, yes!"

Silverman smiled. "Unfortunately," he said, "we don't have any empirical wisdom to guide us in this, because magic and metaphysics are so discredited no scientist would dare admit he harbors a suspicion there might be a power—or powers—beyond the scope of our potential knowledge. This is why I must draw on the logic of fiction writers to support my...agnostic approach. All I'm doing, you understand, is trying to keep an open mind. That, in essence, is as scientific an approach as one can have. You'll have to agree with that much, won't you?"

"I'll give you your first point," said Paul Lawrence, "though I'm afraid I may be walking into your trap of deductive logic."

"Fear not," chuckled Silverman. "If I catch you in it, I'll be in the cage right alongside you. All right. Now let's place the possibility of things happening as the boys have described them on a side-track for a moment. Let's label it 'POSSIBLE, BUT IMPROBABLE.' Okay?"

"Okay."

"Now, I'll go to another of my favorite men of wisdom…one who's lasted well into adulthood. Ever read Robert Heinlein?"

Dr. Lawrence nodded. "Some," he said.

"Well, Heinlein has done quite a bit of writing in fictional metaphysics, but he makes some points that might apply here. Essentially, I think, he agrees with Doyle, but carries his logic a step further: *If you don't know what you're dealing with, you can't say it's impossible. To prove that such-and-such couldn't happen yesterday is not valid evidence to say it absolutely can't happen tomorrow.* That's far from an exact quote, but I think you'll get the idea."

"You're playing with words," replied Dr. Lawrence.

"All logic is playing with words," countered Silverman. "But hear me out. There are certain aspects in what has happened here that bear a peculiar relevance to several well-documented case of inexplicable phenomena."

"I take it that should read 'ghost stories,'" Lawrence said coldly. Despite his own uncertainty, he took a perverse satisfaction in rejecting Silverman's willingness to except what lay beyond the obvious…beyond the known.

"As you will," admitted the anthropologist. "But there are a good many intelligent men—qualified men in various fields of science and technology—who'll tell you they simply do not know if this or that mystical experience is possible. In other words, they refuse to reject the possibility on just the basis of prejudicial past associations with measured quantities."

Dr. Lawrence remained silent, although Silverman was obviously waiting for some response. "I'm listening," he said at length.

"All right. Taking it from here, and leaving the mystical possibilities in abeyance, what can we definitely reject?"

Dr. Lawrence grunted, shifting his position and looking helplessly at the other man. "You disarm me by your arbitrary restriction on common sense," he said, "but I suppose I'd reject the hysterical nature of any physical marks on the subjects' bodies." He admitted this grudgingly, aware that Silverman was following the same train of logic.

"Good. That's a start," replied the other brightly, eagerly really. "But having rejected this, what would you postulate as an explanation?"

"Self-mutilation, perhaps," answered the doctor slowly, "...that or some interaction, maybe of a sexual nature..." He broke off, realizing he was treading dangerously close to an area he wished to avoid.

But Silverman leaped on it, reacting with no indication of surprise. His expression remained intense, but otherwise impassive. "In other words you think some kind of sadomasochistic sexual rite could account for the marks?"

"I would call it a vague possibility," admitted the doctor. "My greatest hesitancy stems from the fact that *both* of them are marked, and in a similar manner.

77

This would imply some type of mutual flagellation… and use of restraints. That is not…er, typical."

"How familiar are you with these varieties of… homosexual behavior?" Silverman asked bluntly. He glanced up sharply, impaling Paul Lawrence with a hard, unflinching stare.

"I…I'm a psychiatrist," Lawrence answered softly. "It's my business to be…at least aware of these things."

A suggestion of satisfaction, or triumph, revealed itself in Silverman's expression. "I think we might clarify one point," he said evenly, "especially as you— as you say—are a psychiatrist." He watched the doctor for another few moments before he continued. "I am a homosexual…practicing, exclusive…compulsive, maybe. Nor am I particularly unhappy about it." His words were a flat expression of fact, not even a challenge. His gaze never faltered as he maintained his firm eye-contact with the other man.

"I…I'm a bit at a loss…" muttered Dr. Lawrence. He poked a finger under his collar and scratched the side of his neck. It was a self-conscious gesture, and by Silverman's expression he realized the doctor's discomfort. "I take it," he said slowly, "that I am supposed to register some degree of surprise."

"Not at all," laughed Silverman. "I had more or less expected Ken…er, O'Conner might already have communicated the fact."

"O'Conner is aware of your…of this?" Now he was surprised, and it was difficult not to project it.

"Let's say I make a practice of hiring those who might otherwise find difficulty in obtaining a position. Not that Ken has any kind of police record, nothing like that. Still, there is sufficient prejudice in the 'straight' world that I like to employ men of my own persuasion, and enjoy giving them the additional freedom of not having to fear for their jobs if trouble should ever arise. Call it my one, small contribution to 'the cause.'" He seemed almost smug.

"I hesitate to violate the confidences of a patient..."

"I'm not asking you to publicize what either of your patients has told you," urged Silverman. "I simply lay the facts before you and leave the rest to your discretion. I would add, though, that if we are to work together—as I hope we will—to solve this mystery, we would do better to level with one another." Again, he waited for Dr. Lawrence to agree or dispute his point.

"You make a strong case," agreed the doctor. "If, as you say, we are to work together." He paused thoughtfully. "All right," he said at length. "As long as you're aware of the situation, I suppose I can go along with you. You are, or do have a certain professional...status. Yes, both Ken and Masten have admitted to certain acts...together...in the Egyptian room at your museum. In some way, they seem to feel these are connected with what they believe has happened to them."

Silverman remained impassive, obviously deep in his own thoughts rather than anticipating Dr. Lawrence's further remarks—or admissions. It was a long, protracted period of silence before he spoke again. "And you, doctor?" he almost whispered.

"And me?" replied Paul. He grinned then, knowing his companion had scored a major point in their verbal contest. "I'm as gay as all the rest of you," he sighed. "So.... Tell you what, meet me back here about eight tonight, and we'll go over the tape together. But..."

"I know," said Silverman, gliding easily to his feet. "Not a word shall I leak to anyone…not even your…"

"Warden," laughed the doctor. "No. Above all not to her."

"See you at eight."

Chapter 7

Tape File No. 701: MASTEN, Gregory K.

(Under narco-hypnosis)

I waited for Ken outside the museum, sitting on a bench in the park that surrounded the building. I wasn't really sure that had happened to me. Now it was over, my reaction was much as Ken's had been following his first experience. It seemed like a dream; yet, despite its short duration it was too real for me simply to ignore. I mean, I couldn't go on from here, saying: "Maybe it happened; maybe it didn't." The uncertainty would have haunted me all the rest of my life. Even then, I knew I had to find a better answer.

From the short conversation we had had before I left the museum, I knew his recollections were exactly the same as mine. He confirmed everything I had seen and done…felt, in precise detail. I couldn't understand it or explain it. I only knew I could not reject it out-of-hand. The exotic scent of myrrh and cassia still filled my nostrils, and I could feel the heavy layer of oil adhering to my skin.

When Ken finally came out he was dressed in jeans and a blue polo shirt, with a nylon jacket open down the front. It was still early, and there was a light, misty fog hanging close to the ground that would not lift for another hour, or so; but already a number of people were drifting into the park. I guess it was a gathering place for senior citizens, but while we sat talking no one seemed to pay much of any attention to us—not like they might have, if Ken had been wearing his uniform.

As I said, I had done some thinking while I waited for my friend, so I was ready with a lot more questions, and suggested explanations, by the time he joined me. But most of these had been such wild flights of fancy, I recanted in my own mind before I ever said them. Somehow, the reality of Ken's sitting beside me forced my mind to reaffirm what I had almost rejected during the short interim of our separation. Thus, it was several minutes before I said anything at all. He was watching me with a concerned expression, so I finally looked at him and forced a smile. "It really *did* happen, didn't it?" I asked uncertainly.

"If you think it did, and I think it did…it must have," he told me. "But you're the brain. Got any ideas?"

"This isn't something they prepare you to understand in school," I said defensively. "Is that why you…took me…there? You thought I could explain it?"

"No, not really," he said slowly. "I think it was more because I wasn't sure I'd been where I thought

I'd been. Even now…both times, I mean…even now, it seems…I'm not sure."

"Maybe we should go back again," I suggested. I tried to make my tone doubtful, as if I were not sure. But before I'd finished the sentence, Ken knew I meant it—and so I did. I wanted to see that place again—had to see it!

Ken didn't look confident at all. He's dark and swarthy, but as I told him this he got even darker. When he spoke, though, his voice was soft and controlled. "We were lucky this last trip," he told me. "We came out in a good place, not like I did before. Only trouble is, there doesn't seem to be any way to tell where you'll land."

"There probably is, if we could figure it out," I suggested.

Again, Ken deferred to me. "Okay," he said. "What do you think made me land in two different places… once before the idol, once outside on the sand?"

"I think you actually went in the direction of the idol both times. Once, for some reason, you were 'short-stopped.' I mean, you were stopped by the sand, but you were still on the hillside, probably right over the hall where the idol was."

"In other words, I was going in the same direction, and…"

"And another thing," I added. "The time lapse between your two trips seems the same on both ends. Remember? Nebnofer said you had been there two days before. I don't know just how to say it, but I wonder if you're not being called back there to do…something."

"To do what? For who?" he asked.

I shook my head. "I don't know," I admitted. "I'm no more qualified to figure this out than you are, and if I try to ask someone to help us he'll think we're both freaked-out on something. But while I've been waiting for you, I have done a little thinking."

"That figures. What'd you come up with?"

"Well, for one thing," I said, "there isn't any reason for us to go unarmed…if we do go back. And I don't see why we should have to go through naked." I pulled open the collar on my shirt. "Can you see the oil on me?" I asked. "I can feel it…and smell it." I saw Ken nodding. "Well, this was put on me in…*there*, and it's still on me. It came through with me."

"Through?"

I shrugged. "It's the best way I can think to express it," I said. "We passed through time and across space…unless we want to deny it happened at all."

"Guess we can't do that," he agreed. "But do you think we could really take clothes and…what, a gun?"

"I don't see why not. As long as whatever we take is on our bodies…a part of us, so to speak. I'm sure it'd go through…whatever it is we're passing through."

"Maybe," said Ken doubtfully. "But have you thought…? What I'm trying to say is, if we go armed we're asking someone to shoot at us—arrows or spears, maybe. But I've got a hunch if one of them mothers connected, we'd be just as dead as if it happened right here!"

I got thoughtful, because he made sense, and it started me on still another step ahead. "That's true," I agreed, "and not only that. We'd have to be damned careful we didn't kill anyone. If we did, God knows how many people it might mean we murdered."

Ken looked puzzled, obviously not understanding me. "I mean," I explained, "if we really were...are going back thirty-five hundred years, and we kill a man—just one man—imagine how may thousands of descendants we might cork right there—people who'll never be born, because we prevented the man from breeding. And how many more thousands...millions, maybe, might we alter? I mean, if the descendants of the one we kill aren't around to woo fair maid, someone else is going to. So, the children she might have had by him, she'd maybe have by someone else. Only they wouldn't be the same. Nor will their children, or their children's children. One thing we learned in genetics...a simple statistic, but one you might not think of if someone didn't point it out to you.... It's like the old story of the wise-acre who conned his boss into hiring him for a penny a day, and doubling his salary every succeeding day. At the end of a month he owned the world. It's the same with generations of offspring. If a couple have two children, and each of them has two, and two, and two...in thirty generations, figure how many descendants that is. And between the time we're apparently in...when we pass through whatever we pass through, and now.... That leaves enough room for a lot more than thirty generations."

Ken had listened quietly to my tirade, and surprised me by adding an embellishment I hadn't thought of. "And if just one of those thousands...maybe millions of descendants ever became important enough to change something in history...well, if things suddenly didn't work out the way we know them, we might find ourselves in ancient Egypt with no way to get back—because there might not be any 'back.'"

"Now you're with it!" I replied enthusiastically.

"But if we do it again, I still think we outta be armed," he continued. "We could shoot for the big toe, or something."

I agreed with him, and we decided to meet back at the museum that night. Ken had a gun, of course. It was part of his guard uniform. In addition to whatever else Dr. Silverman had in his building, the rubies in the idol's eyes were real—and huge! I'd hate to think what they'd cost in a Beverly Hills jewelry shop!

We didn't try to fathom the "why" of it any more just then; both of us were too tired. I would liked to have slept with Ken, but I was staying with friends of Dr. Summerfield; and he lived in a rooming house. Maybe it was just as well, because we'd probably have kept on talking…or done things. Anyway, neither of us would have gotten any sleep.

We were both on our knees, sideways to the idol. It had been drizzling all afternoon, so there was a clammy chill in the air—even inside the building. This, in addition to the fact we were not engaging in a completely spontaneous act, got us off to a slow start.

I can't speak for Ken, but to me there was more a feeling of affection than blatant sex in what we did, and it was this that started the old engine turning. In the beginning we were both covered with goose-bumps, and like I said we were actors on a stage through those first few minutes. But Ken was running his hands over my shoulders and back; I was doing the same to him. Our kisses quickly assumed more meaning, and the whispered remarks between them were very real. This was the first indication Ken had given to acknowledge any reciprocation of my feelings toward him.

Pressed against him, feeling his naked, hairy form touching me from head to knee-cap, I forgot all about the chill air that surrounded us, or the light rain falling outside. I even ignored the twinkling, ruby eyes, staring down at us, observing all we did. As I held Ken tightly to me, I told him outright that I loved him. His face was beside mine at that point, my mouth less than an inch from his ear. I couldn't see the expression on his face, but I felt a responding quiver course through his body. The grip of his arms about me became tighter, and his fists pressed more deeply into my back.

For a moment he didn't say anything, just held me. I was afraid I might have over-stepped what he perceived as the limits of our relationship. Although we had already shared a fantastic adventure together, we had actually only been in each other's company twice. To admit I loved him so quickly might very well have had a negative effect. I hardly dared breathe until I felt the movement of his lips against the side of my head, and heard his voice whispering in my ear. "I love you, too," he told me. "Yes, I do love you!"

Our lips came together again, and we slowly sank onto the soft surface of the deep, Persian rug. Ken shoved me gently onto my back, lying on top of me, his cock a hard, jutting pole pressing furiously against my stomach. Hotly, wetly, he kissed my mouth, my eyes, worked his way down to my neck, where he fastened his teeth against the skin, pulling it into him, laving it with his tongue. I know he was probably leaving marks around my throat, but I didn't care. I would willingly have allowed him to do anything he wanted, and without expressing it in words he seemed to realize this. His arms slipped beneath me, and his head dropped down to my chest where his lips grasped first one nipple, then the other—chewing on them as he had on my neck, drawing the flesh into his mouth, pinching the hardened tips between his teeth.

As Ken had moved his body lower on mine, I felt his cock travel past my groin, finally settling itself between my thighs. Now, as he worked on my tits I felt the softer covering of his cockhead pressing into the underside of my crotch. Like the iron hand in the velvet glove, his rod jabbed my prostate through the padded bulb. Fierce sensations of tremendous depth and magnitude flooded my viscera. I remember only a single, fleeting moment when I was aware enough of my environment to consciously hope that whatever the mysterious force had been, it would restrain its interference, and permit us the full expression of dark passageway, stumbling over each other in the framework of more than physical lust.

I had already considered the possibility of our location within the "real" world being a determinant of the area in which we would emerge if and when the god should decide to transport us for a second time. Ken had placed the rug in the exact position where it had been before, and I hoped its terminus would prove the same as it had on the previous occasion. Now, I was thinking no more about it. Despite the fact our very lives might depend upon our point of exit, nothing mattered but the hard, firm body that pressed down upon me. I was only aware of his being, and of the fleshy sex that was beginning to pump in a steady, regular rhythm between my legs.

I closed my eyes and allowed him to take complete possession. I made no move to slow him or to prevent his total penetration. My own cock was pressed hard between our straining midsections, and I was experiencing a thrill that bordered release. Ken beat faster and faster against me, his breath coming in sharper, deeper gasps beside my ear.

"I'm coming!" he whispered at last. "I'm going to pound it into you, baby! Ask me now if I love you… ask me now!" He started to shoot, and waves of wild sensation mingled with flashes of blue. Cold, shimmering light enveloped us as Ken fired his load deep inside me.

It had not been the smooth transition it was before. Though fiercely intense and…jagged, there was no sound and the blue lightning seemed to grapple with us, as if the force didn't have as sure a grip. We were tossed like driftwood in a heavy surf, and I felt pressure against me…so strong I was unable to catch my breath for several seconds. Then we were bathed in a brilliant, searing glare—red and almost painful after the cold, cobalt fires that had carried us up from the museum floor. We were dumped—dropped as if from a height of several feet—upon sand so white it seemed bleached by the rays of sunlight.

"Shit!" growled Ken. "Look where we came out!"

I was struggling to keep my eyes open in the blinding flood of light. Squinting through the partial shade of my lashes I could see the outline of an open tent, sort of striped pavilion. We seemed to be near the crest of a long, gradual rise. As my pupils adjusted to the brilliance, I made out the forms of two men. They stood in the doorway, staring down at us. "That's Paneb," said Ken from behind me. "The other one's the captain of the guard."

Before I could reply, one of the men—Paneb, I think, though I could not see clearly enough to be sure—started shouting frantically for the soldiers. "Seize them! Seize them!" he bellowed. "Escaped slaves! Seize them!"

Ken was standing by then, and I was still on my knees, not sure I would keep my balance if I got up. I felt his hand under my armpit, lifting me. "You okay?" he muttered. "Hurry up. They're almost..."

"Don't shoot!" I reminded him. My gaze had focused enough to see the revolver in his hand. Behind him were a dozen men with spears—and little else—struggling up the hill.

"Just the noise might scare them," Ken replied.

I was on my feet, then, fear forcing my body to adjust. "Wait!" I shouted. I held my hand out, like a traffic cop. "Don't pull the trigger just yet," I whispered. "Let's make it dramatic."

"Dramatic, shit!" insisted Ken. "I could drop Paneb right now."

"And all his thousands of descendants...and Christ knows how much of history," I reminded him.

While we spoke the soldiers moved a few feet closer up the hill, apparently waiting for their officers to urge them on. Both men in the tent were gaping at us, however, seeing Ken holding the gun and apparently wondering what it was. The white kilts of the soldiers blurred into a blinding row of white, as they finally came to a halt. Then Paneb screamed at them again, and started toward us.

"The tentpole!" I shouted to Ken. "If you hit it…"

CRACK! He'd needed no further urging. The gun roared in his hand, the sharp report echoing off the hills behind us. His bullet splintered the wooden upright which supported a cross-beam above the door. The entire pavilion sagged on its front side. This dropped a wall of cloth between us and the two officers, the overhang catching Paneb across the middle of his chest. I could see the outline of someone beating against the material, while he shouted in rage and confusion. The soldiers stopped dead in their tracks, gaping at us in open-mouthed awe.

"Let's get rid of them mothers!" laughed Ken. He held the pistol above his head and fired another shot, lunging forward with his body as he did so. This was enough to panic the spearmen. The front rank turned, bowling over their companions in their frantic haste to escape. Their fear was quickly communicated, and in less than a second the entire squad was in disorderly route.

"Now, where do we go?" I asked.

"Ah…over the hill," said Ken, grabbing my arm. "That's the entrance to Nebnofer's god-hall!"

We raced past the tent, where the two occupants were still thrashing about, trying to find an opening in the tangle of wide-striped silk. Before they managed to free themselves, we were at the base of the incline, and had ducked into the tunnel. As we later learned they mounted no immediate pursuit. The fleeing soldiers had told them our second shot had caused a cloud of smoke, which bore us heavenward…into the clouds.

But, of course, we didn't know that. We raced into the dark passageway, stumbling over each other in the blackness, finally feeling our way along the rough, stone wall. Ken had only been down the tunnel once before, and then under circumstances which did not leave him with any great certainty as to directions. There were a couple of unlighted torches near the entrance, but having no way to strike a flame we simply blundered into the depths of the hillside. He grasped my hand and dragged me along behind him.

"I don't remember any side-passages, except the one that leads to the dungeon," he whispered. "If we feel our way along the left-hand wall, we should end up where we want to do."

Eventually, we saw a faint glow of light ahead. Ken quickened his pace, guiding me onto the smoother, central section of the passage. Shortly after this, we entered the great Hall of the Gods. A single torch flickered on the distant wall, high up, behind the head of Osiris. The shadowy forms of the ancient idols lined the vault to either side, seeming to stare at us in silent disapproval as we hurried past their somber, stone-faced effigies.

The long hall was silent—like a tomb and just as frightening. Now we were here, having slackened our frantic forward rush, I felt the first elements of real, belly-gripping terror. In the near darkness, the massive forms had a more sinister aspect than I remembered. Even the grinning countenance of Seth-Anubis gave no semblance of humor or friendliness. The one ruby eye on the illuminated side of its face seemed to burn with malevolent fire...anger, maybe. Osiris, himself, was the most benign, this because the light cast all the forward portions of his form into deep shadow, completely obscuring his features.

We stood directly in front of his dominating figure, dwarfed by him and by the might of all the Egyptian hierarchy behind us. "Now what?" I asked. "We're back where we started, and no one's…"

"You're the one who wanted to come back, baby," Ken reminded me. "I helped you get here; you tell me."

I could hear a tremor in Ken's voice that duplicated the uncertainty I felt, and which expressed the heavy, knotted fear that swelled within my bowels. "Let's see if we can find that door," I suggested. Involuntarily, my hand sought his and when our fingers intertwined I think the contact lent strength to both of us.

Nebnofer and his acolytes had come through the wall, almost directly in back of Osiris. In the light from the single torch, we began searching along its surface, trying to find some way of activating whatever hidden mechanism operated the slab of stone. I was fairly sure which block it was that moved, but it was solidly in place. In appearance, it was as firmly set as all the others around it.

Finally we stepped back, frustrated and helpless. Ken looked up at the torch. "That thing's near the end," he said. "See, the flame is a lot lower now than it was when we came in."

I shuddered at the thought of being trapped here in total darkness, but that did not seem to be the point of my companion's remark. "If they keep it lighted all the time," he suggested, "if it's replaced whenever it's close to going out…"

"Someone should be along to tend it!" I finished for him.

"Yeah," he agreed, "but who's going to come out of that passage…friend or enemy?"

"If it's Nebnofer or one of his boys, we should be okay," I answered hopefully.

"Maybe," said Ken, "unless the old fart really did slip us something in that wine."

We had backed away from Osiris, and now stood in front of Seth-Anubis. Watching the torch, I knew it could only be a few minutes before we were either in total darkness, or someone would come. Then it occurred to me there might be oil in the lamps by the idol's feet. I stuck my hand up to feel and found the wells were filled to the brim!

"If we could get that torch," I suggested, "we could prolong the light."

Ken shrugged. "If you don't think we'll be struck by lightning, or something, I could climb up old stony-face and get it," he said.

The idea didn't particularly appeal to me, and we'd rejected it once before. But it was better than being left without any light. I boosted Ken onto the god's lap, and from there he clambered the rest of the way, irreverently placing one bare, grimy foot on the idol's head while he stretched the final few inches. He reminded me of the color photographs one sees in National Geographic from time-to-time...monkeys climbing over ancient Buddhas. His hand closed about the prize, his body taut and flexed, outlined by the halo of ruddy light passing through his heavy fur.

Ken returned with the torch, and we touched it to the oil lamps. Immediately, the vault was several degrees brighter, which only seemed to accentuate the austere, foreboding expressions on the faces of the gods.

"Look at that fuckin' idol," growled Ken, motioning to Seth-Anubis.

I followed his gaze and felt another shudder run through me. The sneering grin was more noticeable than before, and the mouth curled almost into a snarl. "I don't think it's the same idol," I whispered.

"It isn't," Ken assured me. "It's bigger, for one thing."

I approached it more closely, and it did seem bigger than it had in the museum. The oil lamps weren't in exactly the same position, either. I was just about to tell Ken I thought he was right, when the sound of stone sliding across stone made us freeze. Close to a dozen of the young, shaven-headed priests emerged from behind Osiris. They were silent and seemed not at all surprised to find us there. The leader came toward us, dressed in a kilt of white, royal linen, and wearing a headdress of similar material. He had a small, gold ornament pinned to the cloth above his forehead. The others were similarly attired, except they did not have this mark of rank. As if to confirm our earlier assumption, the second man in line carried an unlit torch, a mate to the one Ken had retrieved from the wall.

Without a word, the leader took the guttering brand from Ken's hands and passed it to the young man behind him. The boy lighted the new from the old, at which the group formed itself into a human ladder. This allowed the torch-bearer to reach the niche behind Osiris. Never once did any of them touch the god, and when their task was completed they came out of their well-drilled, acrobatic tower to stand at stiff attention behind the senior member of their group.

Though I recognized several of them from the

night before, there was not a flicker of recognition in their eyes. Most of the group were strangers, however, with only three or four of the taller boys from Nebnofer's flock of acolytes included in the present group. In fact, all of these young men were fairly large by Egyptian standards, built like gymnasts or highly developed swimmers. And their implied strength soon displayed itself.

I tried to speak to the leader, but he either failed to understand me, or simply chose not to. Nor was there any suggestion of the cordial reception Nebnofer had formerly given us. I asked, among other things, to see the High Priest. Several pairs of deep brown eyes stared into my face without any sign of comprehension. Then, without breaking his gaze, the leader motioned for one of the boys to put out the lamps at the base of our idol. This done, he continued in a slow, matter-of-fact series of motions to order his followers around us. Up to this point, neither Ken nor myself suspected any hostile intent. I assumed the boys were going to lead us back into the chamber where we'd been before, either that, or take us wherever the High Priest might await us.

Instead, obeying a sudden quick motion from their leader, the dozen young men fell upon us. Before either Ken or I could make any move to resist them they had us pinned. I was being held flat against the idol of Seth-Anubis, while Ken was belly-up on the floor, trying desperately to reach his weapon. Either of us was bigger than any of our captors, and in a fair match I think we might have been able to handle at least a couple apiece. But the combination of surprise and weight of numbers subdued us very quickly.

Somehow, it had been planned. One of the boys dashed behind an idol across the hall from us, returning a moment later with several short, bronze swords. With the tips of these pressed against our naked skins, we didn't have much choice. We ceased our struggles and allowed the young men to bind our hands in back of us. Nebnofer appeared from the door behind Osiris, only a few moments after we were secured. Again without speaking to us, he went up to Ken and removed the pistol belt from about his waist. Carefully, he wrapped it in a large square of linen, never trying to remove the pistol from its holster.

"Why?" I managed to ask. "We came as friends." [I had previously learned the word.]

The High Priest shook his head. "While you were accepting my hospitality," he said sadly, "I went to Pharaoh, The Living God, and I told Him of your presence. Pharaoh summoned his captains and Paneb. After listening to all His advisors, the decision was reached. The opinion of the Keeper of Slaves prevailed, and the Living God pronounced you dangerous. Had you not used your magical powers to escape, you would have been allowed to plead your cause before Him. Choosing not to do this, you have forfeited the Grace of Pharaoh, and are condemned to servitude. I must surrender you to Paneb."

"It is wrong!" I told him.

"No," said Nebnofer, his voice still soft and reflecting a touch of sadness. "Pharaoh has spoken wisely. Your own sorcery has condemned you. You do not serve our Gods. Your companion, most especially, bears evidence upon his body." He gestured toward Ken, pointing at his cock where the flap of foreskin hung loosely beneath the crown. "In the words of the Living God: 'The two can only be sorcerers. That is clear. If the one has never undergone the birth ritual, he can only be of a barbarian race. The other must be a servant of Seth. Together, they represent an alliance of the desert peoples against us. They must be restrained and the mark of the True Gods must be placed upon them, thus rendering their powers ineffective.'"

Chapter 8

The tape came to an end and Dr. Lawrence flipped the machine onto rewind. "I can pick this up on the next reel," he said, "but I think O'Conner's tape is more to the point through this portion of it...if I can find the right spot to start."

"Interesting," muttered Silverman. He had stretched out on the doctor's cot while they listened to Greg Masten's recorded voice. "The whole thing centers around the identity of that idol," he added thoughtfully. "Somehow, that's got to hold the answer. I hate to admit it, but maybe Summerfield's right. Maybe the damned thing *is* Seth."

Paul Lawrence regarded his guest with a trace of amusement. "You are willing to ignore the psychological implications...to discount the obvious hallucinations?" he asked.

"Hell, doctor!" The anthropologist bolted into a sitting position. "Can't you see? Whether it's teleportation or whether it's all in their minds, *something's* causing these experiences. Two otherwise healthy men couldn't possibly come up with corroborating stories like this without there being some common cause. Christ, your own tapes should tell you that!"

"Maybe you're right," admitted the doctor. He fitted another reel into the machine and jumped it ahead to skip the part which contained Ken O'Conner's version of what Masten had just described. "Here," he said. "I think this point is where he picks it up."

Tape File No. 702: O'CONNER, Kenneth P.

...smell of burning oil, the smoke from the torches. Greg was tryin' to argue with the High Priest, and old Nebnofer wasn't buying it. He'd got it in his mind we were spies for the other side, mostly because the Living God... the Pharaoh had told him so. I guess when a god tells you something you believe it, even if your own common sense disagrees. Anyway, that seemed to be the way the old boy reasoned it, and there wasn't a fuckin' thing we could do about it. I watched him holding my gun, all wrapped up in that cloth, and I wondered what he was going to do with it. "I hope the old fart doesn't shoot himself," I said to Greg. "They'd probably blame that on our magic, too!"

"Our weapon," Ken says to the old man. "It must be handled only by one who knows its secret."

Old Nebnofer nods wisely. "So bet it," he says.

"I hope that doesn't mean he's going to give it to their Living God," I said. "That's all we'd need. Let the King put a hole through his royal ass, and they'll really come after us tooth and nail."

But there wasn't anything we could do about it, tied up like we were and waiting for whatever the old man was going to have done with us. Greg tried to reason with him some more, but he was still having trouble with the lingo, and even when he did get the words to come out right, Nebnofer wouldn't listen. Then Paneb shows up, and after the two of them talk together for a few minutes, the soldiers take us away. I think Paneb tried to get my gun from the old man, but he wouldn't give it to him. They're still arguing about it as the guards lead us out the way we came, up that long tunnel and back onto the sand outside.

The guy who's in charge halts the troops there, and he shoves us onto the ground, out in the bright sunlight. The soldiers hunker down in the shade around the entrance. We wait about fifteen or twenty minutes, and then Paneb comes out. He hasn't got the gun, and you could tell he was really pissed! He stands there a minute talkin' with the soldiers, speaking softly so we can't hear him.

"Wonder what happens to us next," I said.

"Courage Camille!" says Greg, tryin' to sound real bright like he's not scared shitless. "They can do whatever they want, but when we fall asleep it'll all be over."

Paneb comes up then, and tells us to stand. He keeps lookin' at my cock, like he has before. The foreskin…it really seems to get him! He looks at me with a puzzled expression, then shrugs and calls the soldiers to lead us around the bottom of the hill.

They take us to a mud and stone building near the slope of sand where the slaves were hauling big blocks of stone into place against the cliff. "I thought that was where those monster statues got built," I said to Greg.

"We're about three hundred years too soon," he says. "By the time Rameses built those monuments to himself, whatever they're putting up now would be ancient...maybe in ruins."

Dream or not—real or not, I was getting more scared by the minute. And I'm sure Greg was, too. He always seemed so curious and so interested in seeing everything he didn't usually show it. At least he hadn't up to now. But what happened next...well, Greg saw it coming first and started to yell. He jerked away from the guards who were holding him, and he runs smack into the wall, tryin' to get away. But none of it did him any good. A couple'a the big studs that cracked the whips over the slaves grabbed hold'a him and held him down while a third one comes in with a poker...glowing red, just like a branding iron on a cattle ranch. Without so much as a word'a warning they shoved the thing against the side of Greg's ass!

He screamed bloody murder, and tried to shake loose again. The smell of burning skin filled the room, and Greg's still hollering...and then it's my turn. Man, I kid you not! That fuckin' iron hurt worse'n just about anything that'd ever happened to me before! And the pain didn't stop when they pulled the steaming tip away from me. My hip smarted something fierce! But my hands were still tied in back of me, so there wasn't anything I could do...couldn't even touch it. The soldiers weren't nasty or anything like that. They didn't laugh or sneer...hardly said a word. In fact, one or two of them gave us kinda funny looks, almost like they might be scared of us.

I didn't know what to expect next, and just looked at Greg who was leaning against a wall, twisting around like a kid that's gotta piss and's tryin' to hold it back. He looked at me in pain and hopeless misery, so I tried to say something that would make him feel better. "When we sleep…" I whispered.

He tried to smile at me, and all of a sudden I saw he looked awful haggard. It made me realize how tired I was myself, and I was wishing they'd leave us alone long enough so we could cork off.

But that wasn't in the cards. First me, then Greg, they fastened brass chains on our feet, long enough we could walk, but so heavy we couldn't run. Then they cut the ropes off our hands and put the same kind of chains on our wrists. They were fastened in front of us, with about eighteen inches of chain in between. We were shoved back outside in the sunlight, and marched to where the long lines of slaves were hauling on ropes to pull blocks of stone up the slope.

We were kept with the slaves, fed their slop, clothed in greasy loin cloths. Lousy.

When we were being marched back to the slave pens after work on the third day, a couple of Paneb's soldiers came up and stopped the line. Without saying anything to us, they used their key-wrenches and took us outta the column. We were dragged along a path that led toward the river, around the front side of the hill where the guard captain's tent had been. Then they took us between two sandy slopes until we came through the town to where the senior officers had their houses.

Paneb's place was fairly good-sized, with a rear yard surrounded by a ten-foot, mud brick wall. The rest of the house was brown sandstone. We were taken into the back yard, where the soldiers took off our chains and turned us over to a fat, negro eunuch. He wore a white robe with a patch on it that Greg said marked him as major-domo of the household. He looked at us in disgust, wrinkled his nose when we were near enough so he got a whiff of us. He called a couple of household slaves—girls—to bring buckets of water. Then he stood back while they stripped the loincloths off us and bathed us. They giggled and joked about how filthy we were, and also about my uncircumcised cock. They seemed impressed by Greg's height and coloring…and they also made a few remarks about the size of his dong.

We were both embarrassed, I guess, but it was such a relief to get clean for a change we didn't mind. We could hear the sound of other women laughing and talking together across the wall, and in the portion of the house nearest us there were sounds and smells that almost made me faint. It had to be a kitchen! Anyway, we're standin' out there bare-assed, being scrubbed by these young chicks when Paneb comes out. He's dressed in a long robe with a big collar'a jewels, his face all oiled and shiny. He even smelt good. "Like a French whore in season," says Greg, so I know he's already feeling better, too.

Paneb stood watching us, not saying anything until the slave girls finished and dried us off. They went away then, leaving us there naked. Greg had learned enough of the lingo by talking with the other slaves to ask Paneb about clothes.

"I like you as you are," he said. "Now that you have worn the brand of the Living God for several days, I think it time I make use of the restraint it exerts over your willfulness."

"What the fuck's he talking about?" I asked.

"He must think Pharaoh's brand deprives us of our 'magical powers.'"

"I wonder if it has?" I said.

"It's beginning to look that way," Greg agreed. "What do you intend doing with us?" he asked Paneb in Egyptian.

Smiling like the cat that swallowed the canary, he motioned for us to come into the house. I figured the stud must like girls, 'cause he's got more of 'em inside to serve him. As it turns out, I guess he swings both ways; and he's had eyes for Greg right from the start. Like I told you before, he's a real stud, too…muscles like a beefcake model, and a chest that looked like it should have been on an ape. His skin was dark, mostly from the sun, I think, and he had a smooth, kinda round face—handsome in a Oriental sorta way.

He waves us onto big cushions on the floor, in front of a long low table that's so loaded with food it's like a feast for a hundred people. "You must be hungry," he says. "Please feel free to take what you like."

Then he sits down himself, on the other side of Greg. By then, both of us are stuffing ourselves. There was a platter of some kinda roast bird—goose or maybe big ducks…anyway, they were good! I ate all of one and part of another before I began to feel full. Greg was not far behind me. There was wine, too, and both of us drank a half dozen goblets full.

Paneb's been watchin' us, eating a little here and there, but never very much. He'd had some wine, too, but not anywhere near as much as we'd had. Remember, we'd been brought straight in from the project and hadn't had anything to drink all afternoon. So, both of us were really drunk, and maybe that's why it still isn't all too clear just how things happened.

As best I can remember, Paneb orders a couple of dancers to entertain us. They're a black man and woman—both young, and stark-ass naked. They do a wild dance to just the rhythm of a set'a drums, played by another black kid over by the wall.

After a while sweat's rolling down off both of 'em, and it's sexy enough in anybody's language! I feel myself gettin' hotter by the minute. I look at Greg, and I can see he's startin' to get a hard-on. Paneb sees it, too. Suddenly he reaches over and grabs Greg by the back of the neck, pulls him down against his groin while he lifts the skirt of his robe. He's got a big, soaring pecker under there…huge, fat thing with a head on it that'd make a door knob for a government building. Anyway, he tries to shove Greg's face down on it, and Greg wasn't too sure. He pulls back, and I can see the couple of guards by the door start to move forward. Greg sees 'em, too, so he gives up and drops his mouth around Paneb's cock.

About this time, the dancers are ready to come, 'cause I hear the boy groaning and the broad's sighing and carryin' on right along with him. His little black ass is hunchin' up and he's poundin' it in her, and this gets Paneb all worked up…more all the time. He pushes Greg's head all the way down on his joint, until I can hear him choking and gagging on it. Paneb laughs, and the sweat's rollin' down his face as he pumps his groin against Greg and makes him hold the whole thing…all the way down his throat.

Now, I'm real loaded like I said, and I'm sittin'

there watching all this, and nothin's too steady, anyway. But in the back of my mind all I can think of is that Greg's said he loved me...and damn it, I loved him, and I wasn't going to see that bastard choke him to death! The dancers were finished, and I can see them fall apart from each other, like they're both out of it. And still that fuckin' Paneb's holding Greg's face in his crotch, and I can see him starting to whip around with his arms and legs 'cause it's stranglin' him. I don't know what to do, with Paneb being so strong Greg can't get away. All I know's he's choking and I gotta do something about it. I start to get up, and I'm just about to grab that bastard Paneb, when out of the corner of my eyes I see one of the guards coming at me. He musta crowned me with his spear shaft, 'cause all of a sudden I see lights and...that's it.

I'm falling, it seems, and I hear voices talking fast...a woman screams and someone's yelling in English. "He's naked!" squeals a fat lady in a purple dress. "Call the police! It must be a sex maniac," I hear a man saying. And the next thing I know I'm on the floor in the museum, and Sam's trying to haul me off and I'm fighting him.

"Lemme go!" I'm screaming. "Lemme go! Greg's still there! Lemme get him out!"

Then the fuzz arrives and someone throws a blanket around me, and I'm hustled off to the ambulance. And that's all I know, Doc. They brought me here, and I guess I did act like I was outta my mind until you told me Greg'd come back...that he's okay. I wish you'd let me see him, Doc. Maybe if I could talk to him we could figure this thing out. I don't know, but there's gotta be an answer...someplace. There's gotta be!

Chapter 9

"That's substantially what O'Conner already told me," said Silverman. He shifted to his side, looking up at Dr. Lawrence. "Ken omitted a few points, though, Doctor. I should compliment you. He was reluctant to describe all the details he gave on the tape…about his little sex adventures, I mean. Guess it pays off, being a psychiatrist."

The anthropologist's remarks had been said lightly, but Paul Lawrence was sure he detected a note of pique. "You're saying, of course, that you can't understand why he is more open with me, when you've had him and I haven't…is that it?" he asked pointedly.

"That's one way to put it," replied the other. "Funny, I guess most people will speak more openly with a psychiatrist than with some ordinary mortal. But for me, after all the shit I've read about homosexuality, written by supposedly qualified doctors, they'd be the *last* ones I'd confide my innermost secrets to."

Dr. Lawrence tried to hold back a bubbling laugh, as he saw his guest's eyes stray to the collection of books on his desk. One of the topmost volumes was the latest "What-every-young-man-should-know" by one of his prominent colleagues.

"Have you read what that asshole had to say?" asked Silverman, nodding toward the offending tome.

"Doctor R? No, I haven't had time, yet," confessed Dr. Lawrence.

"Don't bother, unless you have *lots* of time," replied Silverman. His bitterness broke the back of his companion's restrained mirth, and they shared a moment of levity at the misguided author's expense.

"It's too bad," added the doctor at length. "Most psychiatrists only see patients with serious behavioral disorders. If a fair number also happen to be homosexual, and he sees enough of them, the distorted impression begins to build."

"They should know better," said Silverman sharply.

"They should," agreed the other. He turned his attention back to the machine, where the last tape was flapping about the re-wind spindle. He fitted the next one into its place. "Okay," he said, "back to Greg Masten for the final installment. He's not under hypnosis on this, but he was more relaxed just the same. His expression is more fluent, too, as you'll see."

Tape File No. 703: MASTEN, Gregory P.

When the guards piled on Ken I tried to help, but before I could get to him...he was gone! You can't imagine how I felt, suddenly alone, and not really sure what had happened to Ken. I assumed he must have returned to the museum and the Twentieth Century; but still I didn't know, and I felt a lump of fear begin to form again. It was only one of many I had during the last few days, but it was bigger and heavier than the rest.

My reaction was nothing, compared to Paneb's. And Ken's abrupt disappearance created consternation of unbelievable proportions in all the others. The two soldiers stood immobile, staring at the spot where he had been. Then, without a further word they dropped their weapons and fled from the room. They were screaming to anyone they passed that they had just seen a demon. Paneb recovered his senses more quickly and raced after them shouting for them to keep quiet. I couldn't see from where I was, but it sounded like he'd cornered them in the front court-yard. It took several minutes, but he finally managed to quiet them down.

I could have run away at that point, as no one was calm enough to look after me. But as before, escape seemed futile. There was simply no place to go. I did take a solemn oath right then and there, though. If I got back this time, I would never try it again. Whether I found a satisfactory answer or not, it made no difference. I was furious with myself for dragging Ken back, and I prayed he was all right.

Then Paneb returned and approached me warily. "Great one!" he said, bowing. "I knew you and your companion must have come from the True Pharaoh! Only the magicians of Persia have such powers. Why have you toyed with me? Has Sethos sent you to test my loyalty? Oh, the misery I have forced upon you, because you refused to acknowledge my brother-hood!" He fell to his knees before me, and touched his forehead to the floor.

I let him stay there, making no move and saying nothing that would grant him permission to rise. My mind was…I was going to say "racing," but it was more of a drunken, stumbling motion. Still, several facts were becoming clear to me, the most poignant of which was that Paneb had to be an agent of the Hyksos king…maybe even of some alliance between this usurper in the Delta and some barbarian ruler in the desert lands north of Syria. I had suspected it before, but his last remarks confirmed it.

"Okay," I thought, *"if that's the way it is, that's the way it's going to be. No more salt mines for this boy! Play it cool, Gregory…. Play it cool, and you've got it made until you do whatever you have to do to get your blond ass out of here!"*

I had a terrible impulse to take my foot and place it on Paneb's neck, and if I had done this it might have been right in character. But that would be tempting fate, and I wasn't sure enough to press my luck so far. If Paneb was convinced I was a fellow agent and a powerful enough magician to merit his respect…a spy of this Hyksos king—fine! I'd play the game, and maybe I'd get the whole picture.

Confident that I was now free of the chain gang, I told Paneb he could get up. I was able to speak a number of simple phrases, as I'd spent every possible moment with the couple of slaves who spoke Egyptian like natives…were natives, though they had the misfortune to be in the wrong army. They considered themselves lucky, though, because most prisoners had their right hands chopped off before they were released from captivity. Pharaoh had graciously spared them because he needed both hands to haul rocks for his temple.

After a little time, Paneb drank enough of his own wine that he began to overcome his awe of me. The longer I sat with him, the more apparent it became that he held all the answers I desired to learn. And another fact was becoming just as obvious. With drink, his inhibitions were collapsing like the rubble of Jericho. He wanted to toss me in the sack.

The husky Keeper of Slaves edged his ass a bit closer on his cushion, the motion causing the whole thing to slide against mine. Now he had butted the two surfaces together, he rested his hand on the crack between them. Looking at me with the eyes of a dying calf, he seemed to beg for my permission. It was almost funny, and I wanted to laugh. I didn't. I played it completely dead-pan.

As if I were some elegant Cardinal in her red ball gown, permitting a supplicant to slobber over her ring, I grudgingly permitted Paneb's hand to stray from the dividing line of our cushions to the side of my leg, and eventually to edge its way onto my knee. I even poured him a fresh goblet from the ewer, and began telling him how clever I thought he was.

"Indeed," I said, "we had thought to hide our true identities from you indefinitely. But with your masterful guile you forced our hand."

"Where has your companion gone?" he asked.

"He has returned to Sethos," I said without hesitation. "He is even now reporting on your loyalty and resourcefulness." Of course, I am making my words sound much more fluent than they were; but I was drunk, and this is what I meant to say. Apparently I put across my intent, if not the eloquence.

Paneb laughed in wine-laden mirth—having consumed quite a bit since Ken's disappearance. He clapped me firmly beside the groin. "Yes, I have done well for the Master," he boasted. "And what a fool I have made of Nebnofer!" He roared again until he choked, sloshing down another goblet of wine to ease the constriction. "The old man does exactly as we would have him do, and every time he kneels before his gods, he brings their curse upon himself and his false pharaoh! This is how successful I have been!"

He went on after this, babbling of his accomplishment, but he never gave me the answer...the key I needed to fit it all together. I might have asked, but I was afraid if I did...if I expressed my ignorance of the plot, it would expose me as an impostor and result in my ass being tossed back into the slave pens. No, that would never do. Far better to keep quiet and ride it out...learn what I could each time Paneb became expansive, and play along in the meantime.

At the moment, playing along meant assuaging the passions of this over-muscled bull. He was getting drunker by the minute, I thought, so I kept re-filling his goblet for him, hoping I could make him pass out. However, Paneb's capacity seemed unlimited. Though he became increasingly incoherent, his eyelids never seemed to droop. Periodically, he bumbled to his feet and staggered to the garden, where he lifted his robe and pissed into the flowerbed. He weaved and swayed, but he never fell; and each time he came back he immediately drained another glass. "Look at this,"

114

he muttered to me, as if imparting some deep confidence.

He held the empty goblet in front of me, so the light reflected on its facets. It was made of glass, and not very clear...like something cast on a primitive mold, as I'm sure it must have been.

"It's very nice," I said, not knowing what he expected of me.

Almost throttling himself with amusement, he pulled back his arm and threw the goblet with all his strength against the farther wall. It didn't break. It just bounced, first against the wall and then several times on the floor. The noise brought a serving boy, who quickly saw what had happened and retrieved his master's cup. Filling it, he placed it on the table, filled mine as well, and silently withdrew. "Well?" asked Paneb.

I was surprised, and it was on the tip of my tongue to make a remark about the obvious power of a man who could produce such a wonder. Fortunately, I was unable to form the words quickly enough.

"I have five of these," he told me. "One of my men stole them from Nebnofer, who holds the secret. Have you seen his other wonders?"

I looked at him blankly. "I have seen his chamber beneath the Hall of God," I replied.

"He has secrets unknown even to Sethos," muttered Paneb. "But you already know this. Together..." He suddenly threw his arms about me, crushing me in a bear-hug that threatened to break every bone. "Together, we shall fulfill our mission and gain the gratitude of the Master, and through him serve the True Pharaoh!"

Brilliant sunlight flooded the room, and there was a warm, doughy odor in the air...fresh bread in a brick oven, with undertones of some delicious, meaty pungency. Paneb was gone, and I was alone...or so it seemed. Actually, a pair of youngsters stood at the foot of my bed, a boy and a girl. They were dressed in identical kilts, faded green as if colored by some dye that must have washed almost completely away. They wore nothing else, and both their heads were shaved. The small, semi-matured nipples on the girl were the only feature that differentiated her from her companion.

They laughed, giggling merrily when they saw me stir. Before I was fully awake, both of them had approached me, the boy stroking my hair and commenting on the barbaric custom which prevented my shaving it.

"His gods forbid it," said the girl seriously. Her tinkling, merry voice echoed through my throbbing head, and had she not seemed so young and so naively happy I would have told her to go away.

The boy pulled back the linen coverlet, and again both of them twittered like a pair of birds when my cock lay revealed before them. As always, I had awakened with a piss hard-on. This, plus the patch of blond that matched the covering on my head seemed to amuse them. "All right, you two," I said. "Find me some clothes."

The girl ran to a large chest in the corner, while the boy stood beside the bed. He offered his hand to assist me, as if his slender body possessed the strength to lift me from the couch. I sat up and felt black waves flood my brain...last night's wine returning to avenge my intemperance. The girl returned with a light tunic, which she held up for my approval. I nodded and slipped my feet over the edge. The boy did help me, then, and I was momentarily grateful for what little support he was able to render. Between them, they pulled the unfamiliar garment over my head, and the boy led me with some delicacy to the closet where an earthen chamber-pot stood beneath a thickly padded seat. This latter had a large hole cut through the velvet-smooth surface, it's purpose quite obvious even to an uneducated savage like myself. There was a drape that could be pulled across the doorway, but when I started to tug this closed behind me, I sent both of them into further gales of unrestrained amusement. Privacy, it seemed, was not the custom.

After this, I was taken into the same room where Paneb had entertained me the night before. Agana, the table was loaded with food. There were several loaves of unleavened bread, still warm from the oven, and a variety of dried fish and fruit. There was also a pot of steaming mush, a sort of cereal that tasted like oats and sesame, and which contained many large chunks of some fatty meat.

"If My Lord desires anything he does not see, he has only to mention it," said the boy formally.

He stood behind my cushion as I ate, and quickly removed any empty dishes or moved those that were beyond my reach into a more convenient location. I would very much have enjoyed a good cup of coffee, but that was out of the question. There was a clear, white wine, however, served warm and smelling faintly of herbs. It was very good, much like a Greek wine I had tried once. That had been made from rice, I think. In all, I ate more than I usually did for breakfast, and took just enough wine to serve as the proverbial hair.

"Where is the Master?" I asked when the boy bent to wipe my mouth and fingers with the inevitable warm towel.

"He has gone to the Golden House," replied the youth.

"Did he leave any message for me?"

"No, My Lord. He said only that you were to be honored as his guest."

"Do you know when he returns?"

"At noon," replied the boy. Actually, he said: "When the Mighty Re holds his golden orb at its zenith, and the time of His loving light is half expended, the Master will return."

I contented myself with that, and spent the rest of the morning exploring the house…

"Let's skip through here," said Dr. Lawrence. "He goes into great detail about the house and about his trips into town. We can refer back to them later if you like."

"Well…all right," agreed Silverman slowly. "But, tell me; was there mention of a lamp? A peculiar kind of lamp?"

"Yes, I seem to recall some mention of it, but I think it comes up in the part I intended to play, anyway."

"Fine," said the anthropologist. He settled back on the cot and pulled out another cigarette, his motions watched with lip-licking envy by Paul Lawrence.

…when Paneb's friends and associates came to the house. One of these was a shifty-eyed character called Ennana, who worked as a sort of straw-boss on the royal wharfs. He was small and skinny, but he always carried a huge, black leather whip coiled about his left shoulder. People on the streets shied away from him as if he were the shadow of some malignant evil.

I met him several times...on three, maybe four occasions. On all but the last he was fawning and overly courteous, like a dog who fears his master, but bares his teeth to any other living creature. Even with Paneb, he was curt and sometimes short tempered. Although Ennana's knowledge of Pharaoh's acquisitions and shipments was constantly monitored and reported, his greatest value of whatever subversive plot this group was hatching appeared to be his second occupation. He was a thief, not only a master of the art himself, but the center of a large, professional ring of bandits and house-breakers. The second time he came to see Paneb it was late at night. I had been left in the adjoining room, but I could hear them as they gloated together over Ennana's latest triumph.

Proudly, Paneb called me to join them, and showed me what the thief had brought. It was Ken's revolver! The little sneak had wormed his way into the High Priest's secret chamber and stolen it! Paneb picked it up, handling it in a way that made me want to run, or at least duck under the nearest table. He saw my consternation and tried to hand it to me. "This appears to be the magic device your companion used," he said. "Show us how it works."

Putting on the greatest act of my life, I pretended to be terrified to touch it. I backed away from him, shaking my head. "Only those anointed by the Gods of the Far North may use it," I told him. "For any circumcised man it is certain death!"

Paneb looked at me suspiciously, and began fumbling with the revolver again. This time, he had the muzzle pointed toward himself, and one finger was inside the trigger guard. "No!" I shouted, but my warning came to late.

With a sudden roar, and the blast of smoke that smelled like the fires of the underworld had erupted through the floor, the gun went off. The bullet narrowly missed penetrating Paneb's brain, and instead it grazed the side of his head, nipping off the topmost roll of flesh on his ear. He dropped the pistol immediately, and it clattered on the floor while he grasped his head, screaming in terror. Then, when he pulled his hand away and saw the blood, I thought he was going to swoon.

All this while, Ennana had stood watching him, ready to bolt if the God should indeed threaten revenge. At sight of blood, he turned ashen-grey and ran from the room, leaving his fellow conspirator splashed in crimson anguish.

I called for a couple of servants and told them to bring some towels and strips of linen to bind his wound. I then worked on his ear, trying to stop the flow of blood. Like any head injury, it looked ten times worse than it was. Paneb was so badly shaken he was afraid even to pick up the gun from the floor. I took the opportunity to replace it in the holster, and to wrap the whole thing in the cloth as Nebnofer had done. I was tempted to remove the remaining slugs, but it occurred to me it might prove a valuable asset in event of trouble. After some persuasion, I convinced Paneb to take it and place it in one of his chests. I watched carefully, of course, to see exactly where it went. "Al long as it remains covered," I told him, "it can harm no one."

Still shaking, he nodded acknowledgment. "I shall believe your warnings in future," he told me.

I lived in Paneb's house for just over a week, and especially after the incident with the gun I was accepted as a full party to their plot. I heard a number of conversations between the slave-master and his various operatives, but I never obtained a clear explanation of what they were actually doing. I knew they collected information and sent it north, and I heard them speak of the Day of Greatness, which I took to mean the day their Hyksos Pharaoh would invade the lands controlled by the Living God of Thebes. But they had done something more than this, and they apparently expected it to greatly weaken this southern nation. Although they gloated over it several times in my presence—and despite my nightly romp with Paneb—I was unable to glean enough detail to grasp the whole story.

On what proved to be my final night in Paneb's house, Ennana came early in the evening. He bore another item stolen from the High Priest. This was a lantern...or lamp, and it appeared to be made of the same material as Paneb's unbreakable glasses. The lamp, however, contained some source of power I could not explain. I only know it worked by turning a knob at the base, and it was possible to make it very bright.

Paneb deemed this quite a prize, and seemed especially happy that his confederate should have brought it at just this moment. "The Master, himself, will be here," he confided to us. "He may come tonight, or it may yet be another few days. He has wanted to obtain a sample of Nebnofer's magic, and now I shall be able to give it to him."

I examined the lamp, but could not make any more of it than they did. Paneb was so pleased with Ennana's work he asked the thief to dine with us. He had several of his entertainers perform, while the three of us imbibed the usual, large quantities of wine. It was quite late, and I was wondering if Ennana would ever leave, when there was a sudden, noisy scuffle in the garden outside the dining room.

"Out of my way, you fool!" boomed a deep, bass voice.

I turned to look, and both my companions were on their feet before I half realized what was happening. They fell on their knees, prostrating themselves before the open archway. As I watched, a tall, grey-bearded man in a long black robe emerged from the shadows. How he had gotten into the garden I will never know, because there was no outside gate. He could have climbed over, I suppose, but his dignified posture would seem to deny this. He was, of course, Sethos, the famed and dreaded magician.

Paneb and Ennana crawled and scraped around on the floor until Sethos gave them permission to rise. He strode into the room as if he owned the world, stopping short when his cold, black eyes fell on me. He looked questioningly at his pair of groveling servants.

I stood up, but made no obeisance to the great sorcerer—mostly because I did not know exactly what was expected of me. In any case, I certainly was not going to mop the floor with my forehead like the others were doing.

"You...is this not your servant, Master...Amix?" Paneb fumbled.

Sethos looked ready to go up in smoke. His face turned a livid red, and the blackness of his eyes seemed more intense. "You fool! Amix was murdered by agents of the false pharaoh almost a month ago!"

"But...who...?" He looked at me in helpless terror. "His powers.... He could only be Your servant, Master! Who else might possess...?"

"Nebnofer is also skilled!" shouted Sethos. "You have been taken in by an impostor! Arrest him!"

Both men were too stunned to react immediately. This allowed me just time enough to bolt across the cushion, onto the side away from them. I made a dash for the bed chamber, as a serving boy dived for me. His hand grasped the back of my tunic, ripping it off me. Naked, I ran to the chest where Paneb had left Ken's gun, and I managed to bumble it free of its wrappings just as the three men crowded in the door.

Dropping the cloth and holster, I pointed the revolver at them and told them to stand back. "I have the power to destroy you!" I shouted.

Paneb and Ennana stood frozen, each of them having seen the potential of the weapon I held. Sethos, however, had the bravery of ignorance. Despite their warnings he advanced toward me, his arms beginning to draw some mystical forms in the air ahead of him. I didn't want to shoot him, but I knew it was either this or risk certain death at the hands of whoever he assigned to interrogate me. I backed away from him, trying to warn him off. He ignored my threats, and continued his stalking advance.

Suddenly, with no warning, he sprang at me, his

nails scratching at empty space. I backed one more step, and fired. The bullet struck him in the shoulder, and he rolled on the floor, roaring in rage and from the shock of his unexpected pain. "Get him! Take him alive if you can, but get him! The curse of Seth upon you if you fail!" screamed the sorcerer.

Paneb began circling warily around one way, Ennana the other. I could hear soldiers mustering in the yard outside. Then, a pair of them leaped in through the window behind me. I turned to face these new adversaries, firing a warning shot into the ceiling above their heads. This frightened them…stopped them cold as a cascade of plaster came down on their heads. I started to turn again, but at that moment Paneb landed on my back. His weight carried me to the floor…I guess, and as I fell I must have struck my skull against the wooden prow of his boat-shaped bed.

"Hold it right there, fella!" That was the next thing I heard. I twisted around, and faced the old museum guard…Sam, I think Ken had called him. It was dark, obviously late at night. There was no one else in the building, and no sound except Sam's voice. He was standing over me, leveling his pistol at my head. Ken's gun was still clutched in my right hand. "Just drop it, son. Let it go nice and easy," he said. "Don't give me no trouble, and nobody's gonna get hurt."

Chapter 10

Neither man spoke while Dr. Lawrence rewound the tape. It was all so clear and so logically stated... completely coherent, yet...*impossible. Impossible?* thought Paul Lawrence. *No, not impossible. Improbable. Extremely improbable, yet still lacking that tiny modicum short of Doyle's standard for absolute rejection.*

"You know," said Silverman thoughtfully, "there is a theory—not a very popular one, I'll grant you, but a theory nonetheless.... So many things about the ancient Egyptian civilization point to knowledge and abilities beyond our present technological achievements..."

"The theory of an alien race landing on earth," remarked the doctor. "Yes, I've heard about it...read some fanciful theory on it, once."

"Hum," mused the anthropologist. "You know, if the people in this particular era had still be in possession of some rudimentary elements of such a beginning…maybe. Anyway," he said more stridently, "it's a thought to keep in the back of our minds. I think our next problem is how we're going to investigate this empirically."

"That is quite a problem, isn't it?" replied the doctor. He allowed an edge of sarcasm to creep into his tone.

"Any suggestions?"

Paul Lawrence chuckled, hoping his companion realized he was being baited without rancor or hostility. He liked this other man…could find it very easy to carry his positive feelings even further. "Well, I suppose we could make the scene in front of the idol… after you've read off the hieroglyphics, of course," he suggested lightly. "Or would that be completely scientific?"

"I doubt it would impress an examining board," replied Silverman. He returned the doctor's grin. "But it might be fun to try," he added.

Both men realized they were edging into one of those conversations where the joking, off-handed suggestions were expressing their actual desires; yet, each had no way of knowing whether the other was serious. Then, too, there was the question of inbred, or culturally inculcated proprieties—less binding, perhaps, but no less known here than between a man and a woman. In the present situation, Walter Silverman was by far the less hesitant. It was Paul who broke off their exchange.

With a slight flush of embarrassment, he moved behind the protective barrier of his desk. The wall clock showed it was almost midnight. "Now for some practical suggestions," he said. He slid into his chair, adding a further element to his defenses as he folded his hands on the surface in front of him.

Silverman seemed to smirk, but it was merely a transitory suggestion that crossed his lips. "I would suppose our next move is to explore the scene of action," he replied. "Logically," he added with a depreciating laugh.

"Do you really think we're going to find something at the museum?"

"Who knows?" said Silverman. "But you're going to keep going in circles here. And as you say, you can't keep these birds in their cages indefinitely."

"It's a little late to go now," hedged Dr. Lawrence.

Silverman nodded. "I want to make some arrangements ahead of time, anyway," he agreed.

They arranged to meet in the museum the following Sunday, two days hence. Their available time was already getting short, at least as far as O'Conner was concerned. The guard's case would be reviewed by Paul's fellow doctors in their regular staff meeting Monday. The young psychiatrist knew he had little chance but to recommend release at that time. Masten, of course, he could hold a little longer—only because of the police charge. If they were to find an answer, though, it would have to be this weekend. Otherwise, one of the principals would be...*be where?*

He'll be back at work in the museum, so where's the problem? Or will he go back? If it were me, and I believed all he seems to believe, I might high-tail it for the hills. I'd certainly never want to spend another night in that building! Which brings me back to my original assumption. We have very little time.

They met at the museum, and Silverman got rid of the guard. "Now, doctor...er, Paul, we have the place to ourselves," he said.

"All right," he replied.

Silverman laughed. "For as long as we need it," he added. "Don't worry; I won't hold you against your will."

They were standing in the hall, outside the guards' room. As Lawrence watched, Walter Silverman began rummaging through the chests and closet.

"What are you looking for?" he asked.

"O'Conner's uniform." He pointed to the item in question. "See, it's here—complete except for the belt and holster. We have the gun, but where's the rest of it?"

"It's supposed to be in...in Paneb's chest," replied Paul Lawrence.

"Exactly," said the anthropologist. "And it well may be. It certainly isn't here!"

"That doesn't prove much," suggested the doctor.

"No, it doesn't. But finding it might have proved... or disproved quite a bit."

"Still working on Doyle's null hypothesis?" asked Paul lightly.

"That's about it. Finding the belt and holster would permit us to reject the story as impossible. Without it, we must still label it merely 'improbable.'"

"Okay, first test inconclusive. What next?" The doctor leaned against the edge of a table, watching Silverman as he replaced the items he had pulled from the drawers. Dressed in Levi's and polo shirt, Paul's companion displayed the hard, wiry build of a man who led an active physical existence. He was taking no pains to hide the sexuality of his lithe, youthful body, and Paul wondered if the display along his left thigh was deliberate. *Looks like he forgot his shorts. Low rise jeans...should be wearing jockey shorts with them. Boxers won't ride well...waist-band's too high. Couldn't show like this otherwise. He's telling you something, Paul baby! Listen to the man; he's all but given you an engraved invitation. If you want it, all you've got to do is reach out and...Come on, Miss Closet-cloister! Let him know!*

Silverman finished his repacking and turned to look at Paul. "Let me show you something else," he said. Brushing past the doctor, he went back into the hall, obviously intending Paul should follow him. The brisk, fleeting contact added further impetus to the doctor's emotions, beating now within the close confines of conscious suppression. Wordlessly, he accompanied Walter into the adjacent room.

"I don't wish to belabor these points, Paul," said Silverman, "but let me show you a couple of things that came from this same tomb." He pulled the key ring from his pocket, again, and unlocked a wall cabinet. He spoke over his shoulder as he worked the lock. "These particular items have never been put on display and I haven't written about them. It's a little reserve I'm holding for Summerfield and his crowd. Neither Ken O'Conner nor Masten could possibly have known they were here."

The anthropologist carried two cardboard boxes to a table in the center of the room. Each container was about the size of Miss Kilgallen's bread box, and each was identified by a carefully hand-printed number. From the first, Silverman extracted a smoky, crudely wrought glass chalice. "I am not certain this was made in Egypt," he explained as he unwrapped the padding, "but it came from the tomb and obviously must have been used by the dead man. There are still molecular traces of organic matter—presumably wine—inside the bowl."

He held the artifact up for Paul Lawrence's inspection. Whereas the piece appeared delicate and well-designed within the limits of bronze age technology, it was obviously not up to contemporary standards for fine crystal. It was definitely fogged, containing numerous bubbles inside the stem and thicker portions. The doctor was not quite sure what point Silverman was trying to make until the anthropologist turned, held his prize in front of him and dropped it on the floor. Paul made an involuntary grab for the precious vessel, but was unable to catch it before it impacted on the tiles...and bounced!

"Would you care to try?" asked Silverman. He stooped to retrieve his vessel and handed it to the doctor. "No one would ever have realized the qualities of this glass if I hadn't accidentally knocked it over inside the tomb," he explained.

Paul examined the chalice with greater interest. "Christ, what Anchor Hocking wouldn't give for that formula!" he said. "And this is what Masten was talking about?"

"I would be inclined to say this helps substantiate his story," said Silverman. "Now look here. I have one that might interest G.E." He opened his second package and took from it another item that was mostly glass. This was obviously a functional device, a cylinder formed of some twenty flat planes. It was about eight inches in diameter and just over a foot tall. The ends were closed, so the entire figure resembled a squat, miniature pillar, cut from a solid piece of somewhat cloudy quartz. On the upper end was a gold ring, apparently meant as a hanger. On the bottom was a small, flat lever of the same material.

"Masten's lamp?" asked the doctor.

"Watch," replied Silverman, "and remember...this thing is exactly as it was when I took it from the tomb. Fact is, I don't know how to get it open, so I couldn't have rigged this if I'd wanted to." As he spoke, his fingers had been twisting the knob at the lower end. Gradually, the interior began to glow, the light becoming stronger as the anthropologist continued his manipulations. "There is no apparent source of power," he went on, "and the color temperature is constant, just short of 5800 degrees Kelvin."

"Sunlight," remarked Paul Lawrence.

"Very close to it," agreed Silverman. "Closer, actually, than some of our modern, color-balanced electronic flash units. And yet...where does the power come from?" He continued manipulating the knob, and the light increased until it was impossible to look at it. "Feel the surface," he said, extending the lamp to his companion. "Only don't drop it," he added half-seriously. "I don't think it'll break, but I haven't had the courage to try."

Paul felt the smooth, glassy exterior. It was cool, as if the light passed through without a modicum of friction. "Can you explain this, doctor?" asked the anthropologist.

Paul Lawrence shook his head. "But I'm not a physicist," he replied weakly.

Silverman snorted. "I meant, could you explain

Masten's knowing about it. As far as its physical properties are concerned, I had Kaufmann examine it at the University lab—sworn to secrecy, of course. Among other tests, we X-rayed it, because the crystal is too cloudy to see what's inside. All we could determine is that it contains an intricate coil of wire…a gold and copper alloy, as best we can determine. In short, Paul, we have here a physical phenomenon we cannot explain, but one we know will work. And it's not exactly the sort of thing a man's going to dream up as part of an hallucination."

"Which proves…"

Silverman shrugged. "As to Masten, I leave that to you. For the lamp…? Science is a strange thing," he said thoughtfully. "In 1490, the leaders of Europe's scientific community thought the world was flat. Until Copernicus, they believed the Earth to be the center of our Universe. Before Erlich and Pasteur the idea of micro-organisms was a discredited theory—laughed at and considered absurd. Prior to the time a jet plane exceeded the speed of sound, most scientists would have told you it couldn't be done, and until Einstein pointed the way the concept of harnessing the atom was a pipe-dream. Right now, we believe it impossible to exceed the speed of light. Yet, one day…somehow, I know man will do it."

"And in the same vein, you're trying to confirm that our two boys have somehow traveled through time and space to ancient Egypt." Dr. Lawrence spoke softly, but he no longer projected any degree of assurance. The strange, perpetual light gleamed softly from the lamp, where Walter had placed it on the table between them.

"I am merely saying," continued Silverman, "that

we cannot reject the possibility of something happening which we do not understand. I've made certain studies I won't go into right now," he added, "but psychic phenomena have always fascinated me. I've followed many poltergeists and gotten quite expert on the voodoo ceremonies of both the Caribbean area and Africa. All I can say with any certainty is that there are a great many occurrences in this world we cannot explain…but which we cannot explain *away*, either."

"You should have studied law, Walter," said the doctor softly. "You've raised a reasonable doubt. Now, how would you suggest we resolve it? Just let our birds out of their cages? Stamp the files with a big 'MAYBE?'"

"Sometimes levity produces a reasonable alternative," said Silverman.

Paul scratched his ear. "Whatever that's supposed to mean!" He knew very well what his companion meant, but his old set of conditioned restraints still held him back.

Walter Silverman laughed aloud. "You know damned well what I'm suggesting," he replied. His voice was loud, and it resounded through the empty corridors outside the room.

The doctor's heart beat noticeably faster, and a stirring within the pouch of his shorts acknowledged the desire his brain was afraid to admit. *It might prove something; it might not. What's to lose? You want him. You know you want him! Say it, Paul baby…say it!* He heard his own voice, but it seemed not himself who spoke. "Do we disrobe here, or do we make it a part of our ritual before the god?"

"I wouldn't want you to catch cold, running around

these drafty halls in your birthday suit," replied the other. Gently, he approached Paul Lawrence and like a parent directing a child, grasped his hand and led him toward the Egyptian room.

Paul had never seen the idol or any of the display before, though his patients' descriptions had prepared him for precisely what was there. The black stone god was a little smaller than he had visualized, perhaps, and the distance between its base and the sarcophagus was slightly wider. Other than this, it was almost exactly as he expected.

Walter Silverman released his hold and went to light the lamps beside the idol's feet. While he did this, the doctor wandered about the room, stopping to examine the "skeletons" mentioned by his patients. The two fingers were not quite what he had visualized; they were not simply the collection of bones he had thought to find. Instead, they were the dehydrated remains of two men, dried and shriveled through the years, but unexpectedly well preserved by the arid atmosphere of the tomb. For the most part, the bony frames were covered by brittle skin. Though the grinning faces were shrunken and distorted, the flesh between skull and derma had left a residual characterization—more than simply skeletal remains.

"Any idea who these guys are?" he asked.

Walter looked across at him. "No…slaves, probably," he replied. "This was a period of some barbarism, so it's not inconceivable a dead man could have a couple of live servants tossed in with him."

The doctor shifted his attention to the sarcophagus. "And this?" he asked, pointing to the mummy.

Silverman drew a deep breath. "I'm not completely

certain," he admitted. "We haven't been able to translate all the inscriptions. But taking what I have been able to read, and adding what the boys have told us, I would hazard a guess that he's the High Priest."

"Nebnofer?"

"As I say, it's only a guess," returned the anthropologist. The flames were jutting up behind him, licking the sides of the idol's legs and silhouetting Walter's lean torso as he watched his companion. Slowly, as if drawn by some gentle yet irresistible force, Paul Lawrence moved around the granite edge of the sarcophagus and approached him.

Straight into Walter's arms he went, placing his own body in as total contract as he could. Paul was wearing corduroy slacks and a white dress shirt, open to the third button and with sleeves rolled just below his elbows. A curl of sandy-colored hair pushed through the fabric. His eyes were an inch or so higher than Walter's, though the anthropologist stood just under six feet. For a moment they simply remained poised, arms loosely about one another, touching without pressure or display of their need to increase the contact. Paul could feel the other's warm breath on his cheek, turned his head to look into the light, clear eyes... blurring now because of their proximity.

Again without seeming to hurry, suppressing whatever urgency might have driven him, Paul tipped his face to press his lips on Walter's. Immediately, each man tightened his grip, forcing their mouths as well as the rest of their bodies into a more firmly realized reciprocation. Paul's fingers felt the hard outline of strength along Walter's back, the twin tapering rounds of muscle that sloped to form a surprisingly deep trench above his spine. He closed his eyes, shutting out the unnecessary visual impression, allowing himself to drift into a totally sensuous response as he explored the other's body, felt Walter's hands travel lower until they clasped the fully rounded curves of his ass.

"Like a little boy," whispered Walter as their mouths drew apart. "A hard, well-formed little boy."

"It's from walking all those miles up and down the corridors," replied Paul. "You're not under-developed, yourself, you know."

Walter chuckled, kissing him again, this time more deeply and reaching far back into the doctor's mouth with his tongue. One hand remained in the small of Paul's back, while the other worked its way between them, fingering the hard, flat stomach and moving on to depress the rising column that arched in hard-spring confinement. When their lips drew apart once more, Silverman reached for the buttons on his companion's shirt, still holding their loins together by the pressure of his hand upon the other's back. Slowly, deftly, his fingers unfastened the shirt down to Paul's waist. He ran his warm, dry palm across the heat-glowing skin beneath.

As Walter stroked his chest and stomach, Paul slipped both arms inside the span of his partner's, unable to restrain his eager fingers as they met above Walter's crotch and began working loose the metal buttons. With the last one open, the short, low-rise fly still restricted entry. He tugged at the belt, momentarily baffled by its unusual, peg-in-slot fastener. Then he felt it give, allowing him unobstructed access to the heavy warmth within.

His fingers caressed a fluffy mound of hair, traveled

across it. He was aware of the silky, slightly moistened texture as he approached the swollen base of Walter's column. His cock had sprung to almost total hardness, swelling inside his pants-leg until the cloth stretched in binding restriction. There was hardly room for Paul's exploring digits to travel the velvety surface that contained Walter's powerful rigidity. With a slight twist of arm and shoulder, Paul managed to free the bulky rod, surprised to feel its unexpected thickness. Walter's cock was in his hand, now, warm and damp from its own sweat. Of little more than average length, its girth was tremendous. Free of the enforced, downward projection, it filled to potential, pressing furiously against its own covering, seeming to stretch the skin to the limit of its endurance.

Walter shoved Paul's shirt over his shoulders, allowing it to drop until it hung about the narrow waist. The doctor's naked torso stood fully exposed to him, taut and firm beneath its satin smoothness. Parting the material where it touched at its lower end, Silverman loosened Paul's belt and quickly pulled the zipper down his fly. He gave the cloth a final shove, causing all but the elastic-bound jockey shorts to drop past his partner's hips. He felt the doctor work his feet free of shoes, then the slacks. He now stood naked, except for the white cotton shorts.

Silverman stepped back, quickly pulling his polo shirt over his head, and shoving the jeans completely off him. He bent to untie his shoes, and after another quick movement stood stripped before the flickering light of the ancient lamps. Paul had remained where he was, watching, motionless except for the occasional twitch within his distended pouch. Seeing Walter's rangy toughness, the coarse, sweat-dampened skin, swarthy and darkened still further by its hircine covering, Paul was momentarily frozen. This was a man, he realized...not a boy with milk-sop complexion and a firm body that had only youth to thank for its perfection. Walter Silverman was an example of man as man should be, strong and powerful with no surplus of flesh nor muscles pumped-up to achieve a symmetry beyond his body's functional needs.

Walter winked at him, advanced like a stalking cat across the few feet of floor that separated them. "You're beautiful, Paul," he whispered. "Even more beautiful than I'd expected."

He eased his naked masculinity against the other man, holding him in a grip that commanded a response from every quivering nerve-ending. The doctor's body seemed to swell and come alive, to move against the perfect reciprocation of the other's surface. A suggestion of moisture bound them further together, until Walter's hands gradually relaxed their hold and his palms traveled once again across the solid globes of his companion's ass. This time, the fingers slipped under the waistband, moving always in contact with the glowing flesh beneath, forcing the elastic down. As the shorts fell away, Paul's cock sprang against Walter's, burying itself within the heat between the other's thighs.

The slender column curved upward in its total hardness, driving its crown against the underside of Walter's crotch. In its full extension it was long enough to pass completely under him, emerging between the hairy cheeks, where it lay within the heated cleft. It seemed to seek the hidden, as yet undedicated offering. Both totally naked, now, the two men stood enveloped in a flood of passionate arousal that momentarily subverted their original purpose.

Walter, while equally as excited as Paul, had not forgotten what brought them together. With a firm, easy pressure, he turned Paul Lawrence so his back was toward the idol. He brought his palms to rest on the other's shoulders, and a moment later exerted another gently tempered pressure. For a second Paul was uncertain; then he complied with Walter's unspoken demand. Dropping slowly to his knees, he knelt before the wall of masculine glory, looking up to admire the sharp taper from broad, raw-boned shoulders...down the softly rounded planes where reflected, leaping flames created a dirth of angular shadows...to the narrow waist, tiny hips...the patch of tangled black from which the wide, blunt cock projected toward his lips.

He didn't need the gentle urging of Walter's hands against the nape of his neck. With no further hesitation his tongue laved the wide-spread crown, twisting to drive itself inside the hole. The full-lipped flesh parted at his touch, and a drop of fluid rolled onto his tongue, rewarding his efforts. He surrounded the shaft, then, driving himself full upon it, forcing Walter's flesh-heavy column between the taut-stretched membranes of his mouth. *How long? Christ, how long since I've done this! Thought about it...listened to patients talk about it...imagined it! Now, I'm actually, kneeling in front of him...in front of a man, a good-looking man with a wild, full cock!*

Paul drove his face into the furry underbelly, felt the phlegm rise in his throat, coating the cock and making it slide more easily, more deeply into him. He grasped Walter's thighs and clung to him in a fury born of desire and long deprivation. *Never realized how badly I wanted it…how hungry one can get for this…not just desire anymore, a need…real, physical need…like an addict without his drugs, or a man whose existence is incomplete without fulfillment…without sex…*

He looked up, along the flat rigidity of Walter's body and saw Silverman watching him, gazing down in euphoric acceptance of Paul's possession. *He likes it! I'm doing exactly what he wants me to do, and it's as good for him as it is for me. Fine! That's as it should be.* He cupped one hand about the swaying sac, kneaded gently at the contents until Walter's balls seemed to twitch beneath his touch and the cock swelled harder between his lips. He continued to watch until the other's eyes disengaged themselves and traveled higher, focusing on the god behind them.

Then, as if muttering some exotic chant, Walter Silverman began reading the ancient writing. His voice changed in pitch and tone, emulating the long-dead phonetic style of the men whose hands had fashioned the great black stone into an effigy of a god. Paul saw the patterned glow of ruby light dance and flicker against the palpitating skin, saw the planes of flesh revealed and alternately lost in descending shadow. All across the slender, tapered body, thick mats of hair grew red from the imposed illusion, fading to darker black as the tongues of fire receded, gathering strength for their next increasing output.

Holding Walter's thigh against him with one hand, he dropped the other to seize his own thrusting sex. This touch upon himself, the long-denied sensation of auto-erotic bliss caused further waves of desire to course through his gut. He drove his lips more firmly into the swaying, undulating groin. Above him, the strange, unknown worlds continued to beat in regular, unaccustomed rhythm against his ears, while the echo of his own pulsing lust struggled to capture his senses, to obliterate the external stimulus.

His own seed was close to boiling forth, and by the increased determination of the lunging hips he knew Walter was almost there as well. Paul tightened his grip on the iron-hard thigh, sucked the driving cock fully into him, knowing this would be the manner... the position of their grand fulfillment. It was a re-enactment, he realized, of the scene the boys had described. It was the essence of what his mind had pictured when he had been forced to sit in professional detachment while he heard them describe the fullness of their own experience, unable to indicate the desire that swelled within himself. Now, his own body was responding to the full, actual being. His cock was on the verge of discharge and the choking fullness of this other man was about to erupt within him.

Walter's knees bent slightly and his hips began their final, driving spasms, forcing his cock to travel faster, back and forth, in and out. Paul Lawrence slowed the motion across his own slick-smooth surface, pacing himself, holding back until the first bolt should enter him, signaling the moment for mutual release.

Walter's voice formed the final syllables. The grip of his hand tightened against the base of Paul's head. His cock vibrated with its terminal passions; his balls pulled tight against the base of his shaft and less than a heartbeat later the full flood of streaming release poured forth. Paul felt the tightening cords, the bolt of jit expand the passage against his lower lip. He had anticipated the flow before it came, quickened the motion of his hand across himself in the final, split second before he took the cascade of salty, viscous fluid. As Walter fired the liquid passion into him, his own flow was spurting across the space between the other's legs, shimmering droplets arching up and out, falling from their hard-propelled trajectories to form an irregular pattern upon the cool, stone surface.

Their mutual climax had been achieved, and both men felt the sagging aftermath. Walter leaned forward, bending over the figure which continued to kneel before him, holding the still-rigid flesh between his lips. Paul had milked the final drops from himself and grasped his companion's legs with both his hands, allowing his body to relax its tensions, his ass to rest against his heels while he refused to relinquish the drained, depleted core between his lips.

But despite the full range of passion they had engendered, and the closeness with which they had duplicated all that Masten and O'Conner had told them, they remained where they had been. Paul began to be aware of the chill about them. The warm touch of Walter's hands against his back reminded him that their combined life-space formed an island, an animal existence surrounded by the cold and lifeless artifacts of a long-forgotten tomb.

Finally, unwillingly, he released the softening penis and gazed upward, to meet the disappointed gaze of Walter's eyes. He got up, helped to his feet by his partner. Arms draped loosely about one another's waist, they stood before the idol. Flames still licked against its legs, and uncertain shadows played across its black, stony visage. Staring down at them, seeming to mock the futility of their effort, the ruby eyes gleamed in the semi-darkness, and the ancient lips were curled in their eternal, sardonic grin.

Chapter 11

"Why didn't it work?" The killing disappointment in Walter's voice was almost a plea. He stared up at the impassive, taunting smile and Paul could feel his misery. Walter had failed where he had been so sure of success! It was crushing him. Unused to defeat, he could not accept it, and his fertile mind began immediately searching for a reason, for some corrective measure to explain where he had made an error.

"We have no proof that it ever happened for anybody," remarked the doctor softly. "It was just a wild assumption. There was no reason to expect a different result...not really, not on any rational basis."

Silverman turned to face him, desperation making his eyes appear to reflect the rub aftermath of the god's. "It *did* work for them," he said evenly. "It had to have worked for them, don't you see? There is no other possible explanation for what they've told you! They know about things they had no conceivable way of knowing about, unless they had done exactly what they claimed!"

"I didn't realize you were totally committed," replied Paul Lawrence.

Without responding, Walter looked up again at the god. For several seconds he stared at the mirthless grin, and never breaking his gaze he asked, "Can you get the boys out of the hospital...tonight?"

"I...I don't..."

Silverman spun about to face him, seizing the doctor's naked biceps between his hands, warming him once again by the hard contact of flesh on flesh. But the intent was not sexual, despite the responding tremor it caused his partner. Paul stared into the tense, impatient eyes. It was the face of a fanatic, a zealot...someone who knew he must be right, regardless of common sense or the dictates of normal reality. "Can you do it?" he demanded. "Not: 'Do you want to do it?' Not: 'Would it be easy to do it?' Not: 'Is it legal to do it?' All I want to know is: *Can you do it?*"

The doctor considered a moment. Both men were confined in the psychiatric wing, and the intern on night duty was his subordinate. Taking the men from their rooms might raise questions in the mind of this other doctor and possibly the attendants. But no one would try to stop him, surely; no one had the authority to interfere. In all probability, none would dare even question him. Once the young men were in his office, it would be a simple matter to lead them out the front door. The switchboard was down, and the guard would have no idea what he was doing—would lack the authority to interfere if he were suspicious. "Yes," he said simply.

One lamp had gone out in front of the idol; the other was sputtering. Silverman snuffed the residual flame and filled both reservoirs with oil. While he did this, Ken went after the rug. It seemed to Paul that a slight frown creased the owner's brow as he saw his precious artifact spread before the black stone god. But it was a possible parameter in their strange experiment, and Silverman said nothing. Now, with everything else in readiness, there came an awkward moment. The four potential participants stood in flagging uncertainty, no one ready to make the first move.

It was Walter Silverman, finally, who became the motivator. Standing with his back to the sarcophagus, directly in front of the idol, he began taking off his shirt. "Well," he said, "if this old body will make it a second time around the track, maybe the rest of you will join me." Showing no concern over who did or did not follow his example, he quickly stripped himself and tossed his clothes over the stone coffin behind him. Completely naked, he waited while the others began emulating his example.

The next self-conscious pause occurred when all four stood free of their encumbrances, fidgeting about on the stony surface of floors as if afraid to defile the carpet. "So who does the honors?" asked Ken O'Conner. At Paul Lawrence's curious glance, he added: "The hieroglyphs. Who's going to read 'em?"

"Let's have it as close to the original as possible," laughed Walter. His sudden open expression of plea-

147

sure infected the others, and Ken was next to relax his hostile restraint.

"Shit, we're standin' around in the buff like we outta be wearin' fig leaves!" he said. "Come on, Greg; let's show 'em how it's done!" With this, he stepped onto the carpet and held his hand out to the other boy.

With a shrug, Greg Masten followed him, standing so they were sideways to the idol. Silverman snapped his fingers. "That's it!" he exclaimed sharply. "We were front and back to Anubis. The kids stood sideways."

"Not every time," Ken corrected him. "And don't call old stony-face 'Anubis.' He's Seth. Right Greg?"

"If it happens again, maybe we'll find out for sure," replied the other. He stood so close to Ken's naked chest he could feel the warm aura of his body, tickling brush of fur. The rising arch of his penis came next in contact, as each man responded to his partner. Their mutual field of interest contracted to just themselves, their concern for the others' presence dissolving as they lowered themselves onto the carpet.

Watching the pair of nude respondents, Walter Silverman moved a step closer to Paul, taking his companion's hand in an unobtrusive gesture. They stood near the edge of the rug, facing the god. Before them, the other couple was quickly entering into a life-space restricted to their own mutual existence. Ken was on his back, with Greg lying on top of him. The play of sinew along the tall blond's back held the attention of both on-lookers. Ken's legs were bent at the knee, so his thighs gripped against his partner's hips, enclosing the slowly activating orbs. Their arms were firmly entwined, each about the other, Ken's forearms marking a profound contrast...dark, hairy bands about the lightly tanned spread of Greg's upper back.

Walter remained with his rump against the stone sarcophagus as he eased Paul Lawrence against him, enclosing the doctor within the span of his own arms, pulling him into the channel formed by the angle of his out-stretched legs. Because of Walter's position, Paul was forced to lean into him to maintain his balance, and even this was awkwardly uncomfortable. Instead, he went onto his knees, pressing his head against Walter's taut midsection. The anthropologist held him there, simply allowing the gradual regeneration of their desires to build without overt manipulation.

The pair on the floor had long since forgotten their audience. They were experiencing what had been denied them for the long period of their enforced separation. "Hey!" called Walter hoarsely, "Don't forget you're supposed to read the hieroglyphics."

"It doesn't matter," Greg responded. His voice came in breathy gasps from the hollow at the other's throat, where his lips were interrupted in their motion along Ken's neck. "It'll happen without it...if it's going to happen."

"Do it anyway," urged Walter. "Make it a complete test...please," he added softly.

With a sigh, Greg pushed himself free of Ken's embrace. He came onto his knees, straddling his companion's groin. He felt the tip of Ken's rigid cock against the underside of his sac, and seized the hard-thrust column, holding it against the underside of his sac, holding it against his own as he started to read the ancient words. Beneath him, Ken shifted a little lower on the carpet, one hand reaching over his head for the container of vegetable oil from which Silverman had filled the lamps. Finding a small amount of fluid left, he took some in the palm of his hand and smeared it onto the combined girth of their cocks. This made both of them slippery to a point where the ensuing sensation caused Greg's voice to momentarily trail off, and he sucked in several hissing breaths of air. He could not keep his hands away from the course of such exquisite sensation, and he quickly replaced Ken's grasp on the combined, weighty bulk. Then, as his palm skittered along the extended mass, his voice droned on, sounding out the phrases carved centuries before upon the block of stone.

Paul had turned his face against Walter's midsection, sucking at the tight drum of skin and gradually moving lower until his chin brushed against the bulky shaft. He dropped his mouth upon it, pulling it into himself. The warmth of this sudden enclosure made the other tense, fierce waves of sensation traveling through him. What he felt now matched the responses he could observe between the other two.

As Greg continued his monotone, Ken slipped still further beneath him, centering his flaring crown directly under the cleft of his companion's ass. Sensing what his friend desired, the taller boy reached back, drawing oil-coated fingers across himself, lubricating his opening and gradually settling into position above the waiting rod. Feeling his cock in place, Ken gently raised his hips, allowing the tip to penetrate Greg's outer-most circle of resistance. The weight of the taller man came slowly down upon him, driving the shaft more deeply. As Greg felt the increasing penetration his voice grew harsher and his breathing almost obscured the words he continued to mumble. He wanted to bend his body forward in response to the furious sensation; but he resisted the impulse, never breaking the cadence of his speech.

Ken was completely inside him, while his own oil-coated cock rested in rigid demand against the prone, palpitating abdomen. His balls were crushed between his own crotch and the mound of hair, causing long fingers of fiery, tingling fullness to reach up through his viscera. His body trembled with intense anticipation. Ken's hand closed about his cock, again, and slowly rode its length, causing such a turmoil of quivering sensation Greg could barely keep his attention focused on the black stone scroll.

None of this was lost on Walter Silverman, who felt his own fluids gathering once again, while Paul's lips beat more furiously against his groin, forcing the broad wedge deeper and more tenaciously against the membranes of his throat. Though Paul could not see the others he heard their interaction, and in the absence of visual stimuli he responded to the sound. He drove himself fiercely upon the fleshy rod, his hand moving faster along his own, trembling, up-curved erection.

Silverman had remained in place, half sitting against the ledge of stone. Now, he stretched to the side, leaning over to pick something up from the floor. Paul could see it was the container that still held the final drops of oil...the lamp fuel which the other couple had used. Holding the jar, Walter shifted so his contact with the sarcophagus was across a point further up on the

151

cheeks of his ass. This placed the lower portion of his body in a more accessible position. Taking a few drops of the viscous fluid, he worked it into his anus, looking down to meet the gaze of the other as Paul maintained his grip about the unyielding cock, watching his partner across the flat expanse of torso.

Walter placed his slippery palms against Paul's upper arms, pulling at him gently. It was an unspoken command for the taller man to rise. He complied, standing within the span of Walter's wide-spread thighs, his long, jutting cock poised against the other's navel. Quickly, Walter coated the quivering prick with oil, stroking it with loving tenderness, preparing for his own impalement. He leaned back a bit, forcing his body into a fresh display of strength. Following Walter's lead, Paul bent his knees, placing his cock-head within the tightly compressed division. Then, guided by the other's hands, he allowed his prick to glide along the well-coated surfaces, seeking the concealed passageway until he finally felt the sphincter clamp about his shaft, and knew he had achieved the initial entry.

Silverman's hands grasped his partner's sides, their greasy surfaces pressed against Paul's ribcage as the two men allowed their bodies to draw ever more closely together. The long, probing cock traveled further into its heated enclosure, driven on by respondent swells of feeling. Walter's hands gradually reached around him, onto his back, leaving a trail of oily residue as they met and passed, the powerful arms forming a double circle about the lean, hard torso. Paul's groin had now buried itself within Walter's crotch, and their bodies were completely merged.

Silverman gasped, feeling the rigid finial so far within him it sent forth spasmodic jets of almost painful response. Paul was leaning into him, over him, gradually beginning to grind his loins in a regular and more demanding motion. Behind his assailant, Walter could see Greg still kneeling astride Ken's narrow hips, muttering the final passages from the scroll while his companion drove against the underside of his body, bringing both of them closer to a mutual climax. The young student's voice had become uneven, catching and faltering as the great cock swelled within him and his balls were tossed and lifted with each rise of Ken's furry midsection.

All of this, Walter could see as he peered over Paul's shoulder. As his own position against the block of stone was growing uncomfortable, he eased himself forward. Supporting Paul's weight, he forced his partner backward, careful not to dislodge the fleshy bridge that joined them. Gradually, he moved toward the other couple, bringing Paul's ass and then his back down upon the carpet, almost touching their companions. As he settled himself upon the rigid shaft, Walter realized the increased penetration of this new position. The sensation became so intense he could hardly restrain himself. He grabbed his cock, clamping his thumb against the tip as if this could cork the flow he felt building in his nuts. But the shift of position had also culled a new surge of desire in his partner. He saw Paul grit his teeth, tip back his head as he drove his hips more frantically against the span of crotch above him.

Paul reached up, gripping Walter's hips, driving his fingers into the flesh as his body spun toward its frenzied release. He felt the other's balls move against his pubis as the powerful cock began to shoot its load across his belly and his own jit burst with streaming fury into his partner's body. Beside them, they could hear the gasping groans from Ken. "I'm coming," he muttered. "Take it, baby…take it!"

Greg's voice had trailed off and his throaty sighs had almost obliterated the final words. For a moment, it seemed their display was going to serve only as gratification of their own desires. Then the flames at the idol's base shot abruptly upward, momentarily creating a reddish glow which immediately communicated itself to the ruby eyes. These blazed in accentuation of the graven smile, and following in a succession so fast it left hardly time to respond, a blinding electric blue seemed to surround them.

In that split second, a fresh thought seemed to rocket through Silverman's brain. Reacting without hesitation, he propelled his body toward the entangled forms beside them, dragging Paul with him. "Grab hold of O'Conner!" he shouted. And following his own instructions, he wrapped his arms about the young man's chest. His command had come so quickly and so unexpectedly, Paul Lawrence might not have had time to comply had the violent momentum of the other's movement not tumbled him against Ken's side. Abruptly, they were falling through bottomless space, floating on waves of blinding light that had no heat or substance.

They were in the Hall of Gods, a wriggling tangle of confusion during the initial moments. Paul Lawrence was the first to free himself and stand. There was no rejecting what he saw. Whatever—however…it was exactly as his patients had described it. In front of him, the black stone god gazed down with the familiar, detached suggestion of amusement. But everything else was strange and different. While his companions struggled to their feet around him, the doctor thought he heard a shuffling sound, almost too faint for notice in these moments of disorientation. This was followed by the grating movement of stone behind the great effigy of Osiris.

"Something moved back there," he said, pointing.

Ken bolted around the idol's base, but there was nothing...only the blank, even rows of fitted blocks. "Nothing here now," he called. Involuntarily, he glanced up at the torch above his head, again the only light in the long, high-vaulted chamber. "Looks fresh," he remarked. "Maybe we just missed the changing of the guard."

"Well, doctor," said Silverman, "what do you think?"

"I'm almost afraid to say," replied Paul. "Looks like everyone's sane but me."

"Physician, heal thyself," muttered Greg.

"I think we're all convinced," Silverman commented. "Now, all we have to figure out is how it happens."

"More to the point," remarked the doctor, "is the immediate future. Will it be the chain gang or some holy orgy?"

"We're in Nebnofer's territory," said Greg. "I suppose the next move is up to him."

Their apprehensions were soon ended. The stone door behind the great idol slid open. A bright glow of light filled the area between god and wall. A moment later, the High Priest emerged, carrying a duplicate of the lamp Greg had seen in Paneb's house, and the one Silverman had showed to Paul. "So," said the old man, "you have returned! I had hoped you would. That is why I posted a guard to inform me should it happen."

"You know we fought and wounded Sethos?" asked Greg quickly.

"Yes," replied Nebnofer. "It is becoming clear to me, now. Whatever instrumentality has sent you, it was neither Seth nor his servants. Once Paneb's men took you from the slave column, my own agents began observing his house. As a result we have learned many things, among them that you are possessed of abilities beyond any earthly magician." With an obviously painful effort, he dropped to his knees and bowed his head to the floor, arms stretched full-length before him. "I offer you my homage," came the priest's voice, muffled by his supplicating posture.

Several acolytes had come out of the tunnel behind Nebnofer, and they immediately emulated their master's pose.

"Tell them to get up," said Paul. He shifted his weight in embarrassed discomfort.

"It's their custom," said Walter softly.

"Better this than what he did to us before," added Ken.

"We accepted your homage, and wish to speak with you," said Greg. The ancient words came easily from his lips, and even Silverman was impressed by his fluency.

The High Priest lifted his upper body, still kneeling and obviously in some physical distress. "I don't think he can get up," whispered Paul.

Quickly, Greg Masten went to the old man and helped him stand. Walter was right behind him.

156

Together they supported Nebnofer's weight as the entire group entered the passage behind the idol and followed its long, arching curve to the room beneath the great hall. Once settled there, and with cooling draughts of wine in the hands of his guests, Nebnofer offered to explain whatever he could.

Greg glanced at Silverman. "Do you want me to translate for you, sir?" he asked.

Walter shrugged. "I hope you won't have to," he said. "I can't do it as well as you, but I think he'll understand me. Anyway, I'd like to try...and by the way, don't you think the 'sir' is a little out of place, under the circumstances?" He glanced down at his own naked body and then at the others.

The High Priest, seeing this exchange without understanding the words, called to one of his followers, commanding the boy to bring clothing for his guests. He waited expectantly for the godly messengers to instruct him.

"Nebnofer," began Silverman unevenly, "let me ask you a few questions. Perhaps we can discover what it is Paneb and Sethos are doing."

The old man nodded. "I will answer with all sincerity," he replied.

"What are the godly omens?" asked the anthropologist. "Is the future auspicious?"

Gravely, the High Pries shook his head. "No," he replied. "At the moment, they are grim indeed."

"Do the gods seem displeased?"

Again, Nebnofer replied in tones of helpless anxiety. "They have never been so angry," he said sadly. "No act of supplication nor apology seems to appease them. Already, a blight has fallen upon the grain, and our olive

157

trees refuse to set their buds. If the gods cannot be placated, there will be famine throughout the Kingdom."

Silverman now came to a point where he needed Greg Masten's help. The concept was beyond the scope of his meager vocabulary. He explained his question to the younger man, and Greg posed it for Nebnofer. "We do not imply you have done this," he began, "but if the priests of Isis and Osiris were to light the sacred flames on the altar of Seth, might the same results be expected?"

The High Priest regarded him in horror.

"Might as well ask a Baptist minister if he sucks cock," muttered Ken.

"Hush!" said Paul, nudging him with his elbow.

"He can't understand me," insisted the other.

"The results would be much the same," replied Nebnofer in response to Greg's question. "For servants of Osiris to serve such evil, the gods might well forsake us."

"Even if the priests of the True Gods did not know it was Seth they worshipped?" asked Silverman on his own.

"Again, the results would be the same," replied Nebnofer. "It is the duty of a priest to know."

Silverman turned to the others. "I thought this might be the answer," he said. "Do you understand what Sethos has done?"

His companions regarded him blankly until Greg Masten suddenly grasped what the anthropologist was implying. "Somehow they've substituted an idol consecrated to Seth!" he exclaimed.

"Nebnofter," said Silverman, returning his attention to the High Priest, "how long has the...the god Anubis stood in your sacred hall?"

The High Priest seemed puzzled at the question. "Only since the last Inundation," he answered. "Two statues of the god were installed to replace those damaged by vandals...by suspected agents of the false pharaoh, though we never apprehended the criminals."

"And were they properly consecrated...dedicated anew to Anubis?" insisted Silverman.

"It was not necessary," replied the High Priest. "They came from a temple rescued by our army from the Hyksos."

"How long had the temple been in the hands of your enemy?"

"Since before the memory of the oldest man," said the High Priest.

"Do you not see what your enemy has done?" asked Walter.

Silently, Nebnofer continued to stare ahead of him, his mind refusing to accept what this strange foreigner had implied. Two acolytes arrived with robes for the visitors. While the High Priest considered what had been told him, the four men put them on. Finally, Nebnofer's rheumy eyes refocused on his interrogator. "You are telling me what I hardly dare imagine," he said slowly. "But you are the servants of Anubis, and you must know the truth. Still, if we have truly been bowing before the image of Seth, lighting the sacred flames before him in the very hall of our holy mysteries, we have offended the righteous gods beyond measure."

"Undo it," said Greg simply.

The old man shrugged. "Words once spoken…" he faltered.

"You must try," urged Silverman.

Standing, as if the weight of years was almost more than his feeble bones could bear, the old man gestured to his subordinate priests. "Summon all your brothers," he commanded them softly. "I fear we may have committed a grievous sin."

When most of his followers had left in search of their fellow priests, Nebnofer sat hunched forward on his couch, staring at his hands.

"You said there were two statues," Silverman began. "Where is the other one?"

"It is in the Hall of Gods beside Pharaoh's Golden House," replied the priest.

"And the Living God worships there?"

"Yes," admitted Nebnofer, the thought increasing the lines of anxiety on his face. "When He is in residence, Pharoah sacrifices before his brothers in the sacred hall."

"Then both idols must be destroyed," said Greg Masten.

Again, the old priest seemed distressed beyond his ability to express. Seeing this, Silverman pursed his lips in thought. "No," he replied. "I don't think we need destroy them. Knowing what has happened, I am sure Nebnofer can purify the effigies and re-consecrate them to their proper God."

They had spoken—however brokenly—in the ancient language, and the High Priest had been nodding in response to their latter remarks. "Yes," he agreed at length. "To destroy the god might be to invite disaster. There is an ancient ceremony of purification. I have never performed it, but somewhere…in the archives…" He heaved himself wearily to his feet. "Please," he said. "Remain here and refresh yourselves. I shall return presently. If the others arrive before I am back," he added to the remaining half dozen acolytes, "tell them to wait for me. I shall not be any longer than I must, and we shall need the spirit of every priest to accomplish what must be done."

Chapter 12

In the great Hall of Gods, Nebnofer stood before the idol of Seth, arms raised above his head, while almost thirty younger priests stood ranged behind him. It was a seminary, the visitors had discovered, that Nebnofer ran here on the banks of the Nile. This accounted for all his followers being so young. Now, standing at the rear of the group, the outsiders were treated to a display of beauty that rendered them speechless—at least in these early stages of the ritual. All the young men were completely nude, bodies freshly shaved and oiled in token of their apology. And only the most attractive youths were recruited to serve the gods.

Nebnofer was resplendent in his robes of office, however, wearing a gown of the finest royal linen, heavily stitched with pearls and precious gems. About his neck was a huge, gold collar, again encrusted with jewels and so heavy it was only the old man's desperate determination that gave him the strength to stand beneath its weight.

The High Priest chanted a long, complicated formula, first in front of Seth, then down the rows of gods, finally bringing it to its weary end before Osiris. The long, monotonous phrases, the flat sing-song of his voice, and the steady flicker of the single torch had produced a profound effect on all who watched him. Later, Paul Lawrence could never satisfy himself whether it had been a case of mass hypnosis, or whether another mystical event beyond his ability to explain had taken place before their eyes. However, the effect was so profound the truth made little difference to the eventual outcome. As the priest's voice began trailing off, as if ending his speech before the greatest of the gods, the enormous stone figure seemed to come alive. Its massive chest expanded and its arms moved much as Ken O'Conner had claimed the lesser idol had done when he was alone in the museum.

Osiris' arm extended outward, fingers pointing toward the false Anubis. The head was turned to face it, and it seemed Osiris caused the lamps in its base to spring alive. The flames licked high about the impostor's legs, at which all the other gods appeared to turn their heads to watch. The scene made the hackles rise on Paul's neck, but the impression was too complete for him to speak against it for the moment. He saw his companions staring with glass-eyed intensity, obviously observing what he saw himself, accepting it as real.

The High Priest resumed his stance before the

offending idol, and now began a faster, almost syncopated chant that caused his aged voice to crack and tremble as the fragile, fleshly mechanisms tried to sustain all the powerful forces that swelled within his breast. The words were difficult to understand, spoken in a form of his native tongue, already archaic at the time. "The god is speaking through him," whispered Silverman. It was the first any of them had said since the ceremony began.

Indeed, the peculiar form of Nebnofer's chant was no longer like the paean of supplication he had intoned before. He now condemned the evil of Seth in terms that one god might be expected to use in addressing another. The idol was almost totally bathed in the raging fire, and the heat could be felt all the way to the rear of the clustered men. While the flames beat high against the Stygian stone, the High Priest motioned for one of his followers to advance. Without further instruction the naked youth was lifted onto the shoulders of two others. His glistening, heavily oiled limbs shimmering in the intense red glare, the youth was set upon the pedestal, his feet only inches from the sources of flame.

As the fires licked along the sides of his unprotected legs and torso, the young man reached up and slowly plucked the rubies from the idol's eyes. Holding one of these in each hand, he stepped back onto the shoulders of the other priests and stood rigid as a pole while they lowered him to the floor. He turned, showing no ill-effects from his experience, and handed the gems to Nebnofer.

The High Priest raised the stones, holding them at arm's length above his head. He spoke another short verse, then hurled them onto the floor. They fell against the stones, striking between his feet and the idol's base. The vault was filled with the same, blinding flashes of blue that had accompanied the transfer of the four outsiders. In seconds it was over. The men stood facing Anubis, his idol no longer consecrated to Seth. The lamps had gone out beside his feet, and all the other gods were as they had been before. A deathly silence weighed upon them all. Nebnofer stood with his head bowed, obviously feeling the weight of his collar, now the passions of the gods had drained away.

"Look," muttered Ken. "Seth...er, Anubis. He's not smiling anymore."

Staring blankly ahead, the idol had definitely altered its expression. The eyes were dark hollows in its face, and the perpetual grin seemed to have vanished into a classic, expressionless line.

Chapter 13

"Why did you have us hold on to Ken?" ask Paul. He sat beside Walter on the couch where they had slept until Nebnofer shook them gently awake. Now, they were being bathed by the young priests before being given the robes and headdresses they would wear en route to the palace.

Walter stood to allow the attendants better access to his body, smiling down at the youth who scrubbed between the cheeks of his ass, while another lifted his penis and carefully cleansed the hircine scrotum. "I don't know exactly how this spell…charm, whatever it is, works," he replied, "but O'Conner is the only one to make it each time. I just figured we'd be sure to be included if we were touching him."

"Then you think he's the key?"

"I don't honestly know what I think," said Silverman. He glanced at their two companions, standing across the room where another group of young priests were showing them how to fasten their kilts and fold the cloths about their heads. "Ken came back ahead of Masten that one time, so I don't suppose it matters in reverse. I'd be inclined to feel there is an active force which brought us here, and that we stay until it relaxes…lets us loose. When it does, we'll return."

"I hope," said Paul.

Nebnofer, who had gone into his own chambers again, hurried into the room. "It is dark and the city sleeps," he said. "I had one of the priestesses from the Temple of Isis offer wine to the several guards along our route. All of them should be asleep by now."

"Was that the same wine you served us last time?" asked Greg from the far side of the chamber.

The High Priest colored slightly. "Again, I apologize," he mumbled.

Within a few minutes the four foreigners were dressed in kilts and full-length cloaks that disguised their various physical anomalies. Except that three of them were exceptionally tall for Egyptians, they would pass any casual inspection. "You must try to stoop if we encounter anyone," Nebnofer cautioned them.

They left the chamber through the High Priest's room, where a hidden door connected to a long, narrow passage running upward to the surface. The group emerged a short distance from the slave-pens, but above them. They were on the slope where the guard commander's pavilion had been situated.

"The captain has turned over his unit to Paneb," explained Nebnofer. "The pavilion was removed shortly after you destroyed it," he added to Ken.

The High Priest led them around the hill, following a dirt path that gradually widened until it joined a well-worn main road. Behind them they could hear periodic calls between the sentries who guarded the slaves. Other than this, no one seemed to be awake.

"I wish there was something we could do about those poor bastards," said Ken, glancing back at the stockade where he and Greg had been prisoners.

"We can't mess with history, remember?" replied his friend.

"I guess not," agreed Ken. "It's the shits, though, isn't it?"

"Yes and no," said Silverman, cutting into their exchange. "You must remember, the human race has been subjected to many leveling forces throughout its existence. Things that were bad for those who lived through them—or failed to survive them—are what make it possible for us to be alive."

"Would you care to clarify that?" asked Greg.

"I mean," said Walter, "that if all the plagues, famines, wars, genocides and other miseries of the past were somehow undone, there would be so many people we could not move across the surface of the earth. It's lousy, but until there's some other place to go, that's how it's gotta be."

"We approach the city walls," called Nebnofer softly. "We must keep still so as not to alert the soldiers inside the barracks. The others, as I told you, should be asleep."

The thick, mud-brick walls of the town were a short distance ahead, surrounding the tightly clustered buildings. Greg tried to pick out Paneb's house, but could not find it. True to Nebnofer's expectation, a soldier lolled against a wall, just inside the gate. Another was face-down in the gutter a few yards further on. He didn't seem to be breathing, and the High Priest bent over him briefly.

"Dead," he said as he stood up. "He must have glutted himself on the offering of Isis."

Stealthily, the group moved through the sleeping city, past houses of sun-dried brick and into the better section where stone walls enclosed the homes of the elite. At the end of one such street they came to the marble walls of the royal compound—the Golden House of the King. "Pharaoh is in residence," whispered Nebnofer. "He returned two days ago, so there will be many palace guards. We must enter by the priests' tunnel." He led them around the side of the enclosure, stopping before a heavy, bronze-lattice gate. Just in back of this was a thick, wooden door. The High Priest pulled an enormous key from his girdle and unlocked the gate. One of his boys poured a quantity of oil over each hinge, and Nebnofer pulled it slowly open. It swung outward without a sound. The High Priest approached the inner door, using a second key to open it. This swung in, and he motioned his party through ahead of him.

With the gate and door both secured behind them, they made their way down another tunnel to a small room that overlooked the Temple of Pharaoh. Nebnofer pulled a wooden block off the farther wall and peered through the hole behind it. "The temple room is empty," he told the others, "but we must still maintain caution. I do not know how many guards may be on duty just outside."

He took them down a flight of stairs, and touched a

lever that activated a lifting mechanism. In front of them, a heavy stone block rose up and back, creating an enormous portal into the royal hall of worship. Directly ahead of them stood the familiar form of Seth, black stone with its ruby eyes and slightly grinning face. "That's your statue," whispered Greg to Silverman.

"Not yet," replied the other. "Not for another thirty-five hundred years."

This hall was smaller than the other, but it was much more elegantly appointed. The gods were surrounded by golden vessels, and several padded benches stood at various points to assure Pharaoh's comfort when he came to commune with his fellow gods. Once the entire group was in the hall, Nebnofer closed the hidden door. Silently, it folded into the wall without leaving a trace of its existence. The younger priests immediately stripped off their robes and arranged their naked bodies before the falsely conse- crated idol of Anubis. Nebnofer stepped into the center of their group after dropping his coarse, outer robe to the floor. He now stood revealed in the elegant, formal costume he had worn previously. The four visitors remained in the background, near the sealed passageway.

A pair of oil lamps were burning in niches near the statue of Re, and from one of these Nebnofer had lighted a torch. This was now in the hands of a young priest, who ignited the lamps beside the feet of all the gods save Seth. Softly, then, the priests began to chant, while Nebnofer muttered the sacred phrases of purifi- cation. The sounds could not possibly have been loud enough to penetrate the heavy walls, but they had hardly started before someone shouted just outside.

Everyone turned to look, and the muted cadence died away. Before they had a chance for more, the great double portals burst open and a squad of kilted soldiers raced toward them. Nebnofer moved to the front of his group, and held his hands up in a command for the intruders to halt. Seeing the High Priest, the men in the van tried to stop, causing those behind to collide against their backs. There was a moment of confusion, and before the men could regroup, Paneb stepped through their ranks.

"What are you doing, priest?" he shouted. "Why do you bring these foreigners into the sacred hall and desecrate the gods you are sworn to serve?"

"It is you who desecrate the gods," replied Nebnofer softly. "You and Sethos have caused the failure of crops, and..."

He stopped in midsentence, his face clouding in fury. From behind Paneb's back stepped the tall, gaunt figure of Sethos, his arm still in a sling from the wound when Greg had shot him. Without speaking, he pointed to the floor at Nebnofer's feet. From a spot directly in front of the High Priest sprang a fierce blast of flame and smoke. Nebnofer stepped back calmly, drawing several figures in the air before him. The fires dropped away and he smiled bitterly at his adversary. His robes were not even singed.

Then, Nebnofer threw his staff on the floor in front of Sethos. As it struck, it coiled into a cobra, hood spread, swaying within striking distance of the Hyksos magician. Sethos laughed contemptuously, waving it away with his hand. The lethal serpent drew back, collapsed into a lifeless heap of rope.

Sethos began twirling his good arm in the air above

his head, calling in a loud voice for the powers of Seth to aid him. Nebnofer extended his hands straight in front of him, pointing at Sethos' stomach. As if struck by a heavy blow, the bearded magician doubled over, gasping for breath. "Looks like we're winning," muttered Ken.

Nebnofer had stepped forward and stood over his defeated enemy. "You cannot best me in the hall of our..."

And that was the last word Nebnofer ever spoke. His mouth hung open in the shock of death. An arrow had penetrated his neck, protruding front and back. He stood uncertainly for another moment, then collapsed.

The suddenness of the High Priest's murder stunned them all, even Paneb who stared in disbelief at the old man's body. Angrily, he turned toward his men, screaming for the assassin to step forward. Quaking, a young archer moved out of the company.

"You misbegotten cur!" shouted Paneb. "You have brought the wrath of *all* the gods upon us!"

"But, sir, the Master was bested. He..."

"The contest was between them...between the servants of the gods, not some...some..." He seemed to strangle on his words, and unable to speak he lifted his sword and rammed its point into the soldier's unprotected stomach. The youth gaped; his fingers clutched the shaft of bronze, feeling the final beat of his own heart against it. His bow clattered to the floor as his knees sagged and he started to fall. Paneb placed his foot against the youngster's groin, knocked him off the blade. Holding the gory weapon at waist level, the slave-master remained silently in place as the archer's body crumpled onto the stone beside Nebnofer.

"It is as well," said Sethos softly. "There is nothing for it now, but to seize the palace and take the false pharaoh captive."

Paneb was afraid. His forces were disorganized, scattered all over the city and beyond. Both his voice and posture showed his fear, because Sethos was demanding the impossible, and Paneb feared him more than anything else. He stepped away from the dead man, seeming to shy from Sethos as well. "My Lord, the time is not right," he pleaded. "The omens are wrong. If we try we shall fail."

"We have no choice," said Sethos grimly. "We are dead in either case. There is no escape for us, unless you can rekindle the flame of life in Nebnofer."

Paneb still hesitated, his eyes ranging the room as if seeking some means of escape. Nebnofer's priests had grouped closely together, and backed away from Paneb's soldiers. They were close enough for the four outsiders to hear their whispered conversations. "The soldiers are cowed," muttered one of the young men. "If we have some weapons we might rush them and drive them out."

"Only Nebnofer knew how to open the secret door," said another. "Our only weapons are behind it."

"Do any of you know your master's spells?" asked Greg.

"None of us are strong enough to overcome Sethos," replied one of the youths.

"There is no one south of Thebes who would have the strength...except Pharaoh, himself," added another.

While they were speaking, Paneb and Sethos had also been whispering together. Suddenly, both of them looked up with pleased expressions.

"Looks like more trouble," muttered Ken.

"The foreigners!" cried Paneb. "They have murdered Nebnofer. They have killed the High Priest. Seize them!" he shouted to his men. "Seize them, and bind them! Pharaoh will judge their guilt."

The soldiers looked at him without understanding his twisted guile. Dark, swarthy men, they were obviously Northerners, despite their shaven heads and bodies. Finally, it dawned on their sluggish brains what Paneb intended, and they started to move. A troop of mercenaries, undoubtedly in the personal employ of the Hyksos agent, they had no reason not to obey this treasonous command. After a few seconds' hesitation, they formed a proper battle line. Brandishing spears and swords, they advanced toward the group of priests who now dropped to crouched, defensive postures, their oiled, naked bodies forming a defiant, though improbable barrier.

Summoning up the words as best he could, Silverman spoke to the backs of the naked youths. "The only hope we have is to get word to Pharaoh," he said. "Paneb intends to kill us all, so if we don't get help we're dead. Rush the soldiers, and any of you who gets past them must tell the Living God what has happened here."

For several more seconds no one moved within the group of priests. The soldiers moved closer, circling warily.

Although their intended victims were all unarmed, they were young and strong enough to constitute a threat. "Go!" shouted Silverman, suddenly. He pushed forward, himself, grappling with one of their opponents while all the group bolted toward the soldiers. Stopped by the unexpected attack, the armed men tightened their line, while those with spears tried to hold back the naked, on-rushing youths. Walter was knocked down, but otherwise unhurt. Two of the priests fell with spears in their bellies, and another three or four were rolling on the floor, clamping hands against their wounds, trying to stem the flow of blood.

But even in death, the young men had accomplished some purpose. The spears that impaled their bodies left openings in the soldiers' line, and two of their number got through, fleeing from the sacred hall. The remaining priests, including the four outsiders in their midst, were halted by the circle of weapons.

Paneb was in a frenzy. He ran along his row of men, yanking every other one out of line and commanding them to follow the pair who had escaped. "Bring them down! Kill them if you have to, but don't let them speak!" he commanded them.

"You'll never get out of here before Pharaoh learns what you've done," said Greg. "Besides, how are you going to explain Sethos?"

Paneb looked at his master, and his thoughts were obvious. If he dared, he would readily have slaughtered the magician with his own hands, claiming that, too, had been done in the service of the Living God. But there was little hope for either of them if the young priests reached the King. His only hope, he realized was to finish off the witnesses, the priests and the outsiders. After that, he could think about Sethos.

"Kill them," he said softly, gesturing toward the unarmed men. "Kill every one of them!"

Again, his soldiers hesitated. The command was unexpected...so harsh it took a moment to register. Besides, there were fewer soldiers than priests, now that Paneb had detached half their number to run down the escapees. Fourteen priests remained alive and on their feet, as well as the four strangers. Even against this seemingly defenseless group, the odds were not in their favor. And they fought for no cause but their own, for whatever spoils or material rewards might come their way. Only their fear of Sethos made them move at all, and then it was a slow, wary advance.

Keeping a tight circle, the soldiers gradually closed upon their intended victims, stepping over the young men who had fallen. In this they made an error, as one of them passed too close to a boy who had taken a spear through his arm. The youth rolled onto his side and tripped the careless soldier. The man stumbled, at which one of the taller priests grabbed his sword, pulling the man forward, out of line. Another couple of priests bludgeoned him with their fists, while their companion with the sword attacked the next of the advancing men.

"Advance! Advance!" cried the slave-master desperately. But his men were unsure of themselves and not at all prepared to sacrifice themselves for Paneb's glory. They had not expected the naked, weaponless youths to put up such resistance. A couple of the soldiers continued to feint with their spears, or to brandish their swords, but most of them began backing off.

The youth with the captured sword began leading

his own attack. Then above the din inside the chamber, they heard the commotion of excited voices in another part of the palace.

"We must leave," muttered Sethos. "Come, Paneb...come!"

The slave-master could not make up his mind what to do. He knew if he fled the scene he would be hunted down as Nebnofer's murderer. If he remained the priests would inform Pharaoh. His own men, faced with questioning by the King's skilled interrogators would also break. He was frantic. These naked youths and their foreign companions had to be destroyed! Paneb dashed forward, grabbing a sword from one of his men. "Follow me!" he shouted, and tried to urge his faltering henchmen to advance. "Sethos, show them your power!" he cried in desperation. "Strike the false priests with fire!"

But Sethos had run to the door, leaning against the frame to peer down the hall. If he heard Paneb's plea, he made no response. Paneb closed with the young priest who had captured the sword, and started to drive him back. He was bigger, stronger, and far more skilled. Still, the youth put up a strong defense against his vicious onslaught, giving ground very slowly. Their contest seemed to become the determinant. The others stopped where they were, watching to see which man would best the other. But the question was never decided.

"Pharaoh is coming!" called Sethos from the door. He hurried into the center of the chamber, eyes casting about for some means of escape. "There must be another way out," he said frantically.

Paneb had disengaged from the priest when he

heard Sethos' call, both men remaining alert for the other's renewed attack. Now, he lunged at the young man once again, almost succeeding in catching him off guard. The priest responded just fast enough to ward off the blow, and the slave-master found himself stymied by the spirited, though unskilled swordsman. "There is a hidden door in the wall behind these... swine!" he told the magician through the grunts and straining sounds of his exertions. "If you can reach it...lever...behind..."

Pharaoh entered the chamber, followed by at least thirty of his household guard. Both of the priests had escaped Paneb's men and were with him. Seeing the King, the slave-master bolted away from his contest, threw his sword against the farther wall and cast himself, full-length on his belly before the Living God. "Lord, they have murdered the High Priest," he groveled. "I have been hard pressed to defend Your Majesty's temple."

"Why should you need defend Our Temple?" asked the King coldly.

"The gems," cried Paneb. "The eyes of the gods..."

"None would dare!" The King's gaze fell on Sethos, who had drawn into the cluster of priests and soldiers, now milling about in a single group. "This man," said the King. "This man..." He paused, as if listening to some sound no one else could hear.

Pharaoh was a man of about Sethos' age and build, but having come directly from bed he wore only a light robe—no covering on the stubble which sprouted on his face and scalp. Even so, he was impressive, with an air of authority known only to a barbarian ruler. He was directly in front of the black stone idol of Seth. He

179

placed his fingers to his brow and closed his eyes. Without moving or lifting his lids, he began to speak in a voice that sounded like Nebnofer. "The bearded man is Sethos," droned the King. "His evil has infested Paneb, who has conspired to destroy the true gods. The image of Anubis...Anubis..." His voice faded, and Pharaoh seemed to snap back to life.

As the King's voice trailed off, Ken O'Conner noticed that Sethos had assumed a peculiar stance, facing the idol of Seth and extending his one good arm toward the god. "This fucker's doing something to interfere with...whatever's going on with the King," called Ken.

"That was Nebnofer, speaking through Pharaoh's lips," whispered Greg.

"Oh, horseshit!" said Ken. "We're all getting into a mood to believe..."

The King had moved to one side. He motioned for his men to disarm Paneb's soldiers and to arrest both him and Sethos. But as the guards came after him, the magician inscribed a circle on the floor, stepped into it, and was immediately surrounded by the icy, blue light of Seth.

Not even bothering with the formal motions used by Nebnofer, Pharaoh gestured casually with his fingers and the light was gone. "Take him," he commanded his men. "Do not fear his magician's tricks. They are useless, now. Bring the fetters to me, and I shall place them on him myself."

"Mass hypnosis, doctor?" asked Silverman.

"Very probably," replied Paul Lawrence.

"Then, you'll have to admit we're here, won't you? I mean, how could we be hypnotized..."

"Oh, shut up!" said the psychiatrist.

"These, men, too," said the King, pointing at the four visitors. "Take them as well."

Greg and Walter both tried to protest, but Pharaoh refused to hear them. Instead, he ordered them chained and taken to separate cells. "They are to be kept where they cannot communicate," he instructed the guard commander. "If they unite, they may regenerate their powers."

As they were led from the room they could hear Pharaoh's voice speaking to the gods, and among those he mentioned was Anubis. Whatever communication Nebnofer had tried to make from beyond the grave—if, indeed, he had made any—a portion of it had been lost. The idol of Seth remained with the other gods, and the King would continue to worship him as he did the others.

Chapter 14

Laying to rest a High Priest of Osiris required a long, dramatic ceremony, attended by the Living God and his entire court. The lengthy cortege stretched nearly all the way from Pharaoh's Golden House to the flat, desert plain where Nebnofer's tomb awaited him. The body had been taken to Thebes, where it was prepared in the House of the Dead—embalmed, the vital organs removed and preserved in their proper canopic jars. The resulting voids in the Viscera were properly filled with cloth, and finally the High Priest was wrapped in nearly a mile of linen windings. He was placed in a wooden coffin of the finest cedar, this within a golden casket. The casket was then borne on a litter, carried by nearly a score of slaves, his journey ending when he was sealed within the large, stone sarcophagus.

All necessary earthly utensils were already in place for Nebnofer's use in the next world. Gold and selected treasures were left for him, food and wine for his journey, as well as the records of his life and work...these to be displayed before the gods who would weigh his soul and admit him to the golden plains of pleasure. Finally, rather because Pharaoh had ordered it then in keeping with custom, several living servants were marched into the tomb, as well. The Living God had chosen six men, whom he now commended to Nebnofer's eternal servitude.

The first of these were Sethos, the Hyksos magician. His years of enmity for the High Priest made it fitting that in death he be required to serve, slave to the man he had so wronged in life. The second was Paneb, the treacherous instrument of Nebnofer's death. He, too, would serve his victim in the other world.

The other four whom the Living God had selected were there for other reasons. Pharaoh knew them only as outsiders, men who had no reality in this time and place. Even they, themselves, were unable to explain their origins in terms a man could understand. Because Pharaoh could not explain them, he was afraid of them. In life, Nebnofer had possessed the power to command the spirits of men, living and dead. Now that he was embarking on his final journey into the realm of Osiris, the outsiders were far better left in his keeping. Whatever mischief they might have done the earthly realm of Pharaoh would be prevented. And the Living God had every reason to believe Nebnofer's powers would be strong enough to protect his own soul from whatever harm they might do him beyond the grave.

To further assure the safe journey of his High Priest into the other world, the King had ordered an idol from his own temple placed in the tomb, as well. Anubis, the weigher-of-souls, the god who served Osiris, would assure Nebnofer's passage.

A single oil lamp flickered on a table by the sealed sarcophagus when Walter Silverman and his three companions were ordered down the stairs into Nebnofer's crypt. Sethos and Paneb were already there, sitting dejectedly to one side, watching the final preparations around the door. Once the four men were safely inside, a priest ordered the heavy stones moved into place, forever sealing Nebnofer and his living slaves inside.

Silverman stood in front of the Sarcophagus, looking down at its smooth, well-polished surface. "Seems I've been here before," he said grimly. He looked up, into the eyes of the idol.

"Why did Pharaoh put Seth in here?" asked Ken.

"I think he heard just enough from the priests that he wasn't sure what to do," said Walter. "Just as he did with us, he figured the questionable merchandise was better sealed in a tomb...out of the way."

"Out of sight, out of mind," said Greg. "Hadn't we better put that lamp out? There can't be much oxygen in here."

"Shit, we're gonna die anyway," said Ken. "We might as well see as long as we can."

"I don't...think...we're going to die...not immediately," said Silverman.

"Would you stake your life on it?" asked Paul.

"Funny, funny," muttered Walter. "Come on, help me hunt through these chests. They took Nebnofer's magic lantern back from Paneb's house. It's got to be here someplace."

"What makes you so sure?" asked Ken.

"For Christ's sake, man, don't you understand?" asked Walter impatiently. "This is it! It's come full circle. This is the tomb I opened at Abu Simbel! The lamp was in it then; it's got to be here now."

"And there were two skeletons in the tomb," said Greg. "Sethos and Paneb, or two of us?"

"Let's worry about that when we find the lamp," insisted Walter. "It will give us plenty of light, and it won't use up the oxygen."

Through all of this, Sethos and Paneb had remained seated on the sacks of grain and flour left for Nebnofer's sustenance in the other world. Only at the last moment had the fetters been struck from the magician's wrists, and he sat rubbing them, silent and thoughtful. Unable to understand the words of these strange foreigners, he simply observed their motions, waiting for them to finish whatever they wished to do. He already knew what path led to his own salvation.

Paul found the lamp under a mass of crockery, in a small cedar crate. He pulled it out and handed it to Silverman. The anthropologist quickly turned the know, and as soon as the gleam of light flickered through the cloudy glass, Greg snuffed out the oil lamp. After this, the four withdrew to the end of the tomb, away from the other pair of captives.

Slowly, Sethos rose and walked to the idol. He stood before it, and began murmuring a prayer. He spoke for an hour, two hours, and still the god made no response. At first, all the others had been watching him; but after a while it seemed apparent he was going to accomplish nothing. The atmosphere of the tomb became close, and even their light robes made them sweat. As he had in the museum, at the start of their adventure, Walter was the first to strip. "Might as well go in comfort, if we're going," he said. He pulled apart a bundle of the fine materials left for Nebnofer's comfort, and patted them into a wide, soft surface. "Care to join me, Paul?" he asked.

"I might as well," replied his friend glumly.

"Looks like a good idea," said Ken. He made a similar nest for himself, and Greg. In the background, Sethos never ceased his prayers, although Paneb had drunk himself senseless from one of the wine crocks, and had fallen asleep on the floor. Curled into a ball, he snored like a pig until Sethos kicked him, and he rolled onto his face.

"You know, if we knocked those two off, there'd be more air for us," muttered Ken.

"They might have the same thought," said Paul. "Maybe one of us better stay awake."

"I really don't think any of these things make any difference," insisted Silverman. "No listen to me! I realize that a man facing death likes to think he's going out with a certain dignity, and I don't want to sound like I'm any crazier than I am. But..." He paused, looking sharply at his companions. "But, I have the feeling...if the god's going to help us, we're going to have to help ourselves, at least a little bit."

"Lead on," mumbled Paul sleepily.

"No, now...don't fall asleep! I don't want to take time to explain my idea, but I think we need an...an emotional output...all of us..."

Ken whooped in laughter, which startled Sethos so

he stopped his prayer and glanced around. Paneb merely grunted in his sleep and rolled onto his back. "You saying we should have sex? Suck and fuck right here…in the old man's tomb?"

Silverman nodded seriously. "Yes," he said quietly. "That is exactly what I mean."

"Nothing like dying happy!" Greg remarked.

"Well, maybe it's our last chance," said Paul Lawrence. He regarded Walter intently, fondly. "I guess I can't think of a more pleasant way to go," he agreed. "And just for the record," he added meaningfully, "I think you're probably right."

Ken and Greg both looked puzzled, but if their two companions thought it was okay…

"And just remember," added Paul as he grasped Walter's cock, lips poised above its gleaming surface. "Nebnofer's trick with the staff—turning it into a snake…that was in the bible. Moses did it." And with that curious rejoinder, he sucked the entire shaft into his mouth, thus precluding any further conversation.

Ken shrugged. "I don't know what the fuck he's talking about, but here goes!" He pulled Greg against him, twisting his body so he lay on top of the taller man. Enforced separation had again resulted in a level of desire which transcended their inhibiting circumstances. Their hard, driving bodies moved in fully reciprocating voluption. Their faces were bearded now, because of the long wait for Nebnofer's body to be prepared. Ken's shaggy visage worked against Greg's chest and neck, until his friend swung himself around, bringing his mouth down on Ken's gnarled, pulsing cock. He felt his partner's lips close about his own, as they pulled tightly against each other, their lustful expectancy building toward an emotional peak.

Between Paul and Walter, a similar merging was starting them toward their own outpouring of feeling. Instead of the passionate, writhing sixty-nine, however, they lay face-to-face, bodies closely compressed as they rocked gently back and forth upon the softness of fine silks and linens. Their mouths never seemed to part, nor their arms to relinquish any suggestion of the hard-flexed power that held one upon the other. First Paul would be on top; then with an easy thrust of his foot, Walter would topple them so his weight fell across the other...until Paul reversed their positions. Between them, their cocks pressed in a hardness that emphasized their long weeks of yearning. Moist and sweating, they gripped one another ever harder...their pricks near bursting as long-pent fluids surged within their balls, ready to propel them onto the highest planes of physical and emotional ecstasy.

As the four men continued their respective exchanges, responding now to urges more basic than Walter Silverman's logic, Sethos maintained his pleading supplication before the black stone god. His murmuring drone had drifted into the background of the others' awareness, so they were unprepared for the sudden, quick flash of blue.

It had happened so quickly, no one was sure... certainly not sure enough to break off their swelling contacts...to relinquish the holds they maintained against the hot, pounding lust...each giving and receiving full measure...thoughts drawn wildly, irresistibly toward just one goal...the fulfillment of surging desire as personified by the driving rods, the full responses within each man's body as neurons crackled with fiery sensation, casting them upwards toward the moment of erupting discharge…

Cold, blue flames filled the room, blinding them, seeming to arrest their motions, holding them on the brink of absolute euphoria. Slowly, as if moving in a dream or through the heavy restraint of some highly vicious liquid, the four participants looked across to where Sethos had prostrated himself before his god.

The idol was completely obscured in its flashing glare, and the magician's voice was crying triumphantly through the brittle silence. "Spare me; spare your most loyal and faithful servant," he chanted. "Take me from this place and…"

"Don't look at him," muttered Paul. "It's hypnosis…has to be. Look away!"

"No, watch him!" urged Silverman. "It doesn't matter how he creates the illusion. You must see it and believe in it."

No one disputed him. The spectacle compelled their attention. The magician continued to kneel and murmur his plea at the foot of Seth's pedestal. Then another voice seemed to answer him, coming from all about them…from everywhere. "Failure, failure…" They felt it more than hearing words. "You have failed me," the impression persisted. "I have the soul of a High Priest of Osiris to entertain me through eternity…and these others…others…they do not belong! Their presence offends me!"

The blue light increased, obscuring both god and kneeling servant. Each man felt the soft, cloth surface beneath his body start to fade, give way to nothing as he clung in desperation to the naked form of his companion…falling…through fading light…black-ness…

"Oh! Four of them!" shrieked a fat lady in a purple dress. "This is disgraceful!"

"It's the same woman!" shouted Ken. "It's the same old broad in the same old dress! We're back! We're back!" Leaping up, this naked, bearded satyr grabbed this startled matron and danced her full around, laughing in near hysterical glee.

The others staggered to their feet as Sam Fisher raced into the room. "Jesus, Dr. Silverman! My God, sir! We thought you were gone for good!"

Chapter 15

The four adventurers stood gazing up at the black stone idol. The museum was closed, and all the guests had left—including the startled lady in her purple shift. The four had cleaned up and dressed, returning to the Egyptian room while Sam had been sent off for a couple of hours.

The ruby eyes sparkled softly, reflecting the final rays of sunlight, filtering through the windows on either side. The subtle smile remained as it always had been…as it had remained for thirty-five centuries. Ken turned and looked thoughtfully at the mummy. "If that's Nebnofer," he said, "I wonder what he'd think of all this."

"It would be interesting to know how much his…I hesitate to say 'spirit,' but we don't have a better word in English. Whatever you want to call it, I wonder how much it had to do with all that happened to us," said Paul Lawrence.

"I'd say a great deal," replied Silverman. "But I wonder if he's really at peace...or Sethos, either, for that matter," he added, glancing at the pair of skeletons with their parchment-like coverings.

"Can you tell which is which?" asked Ken.

"That wouldn't be very hard," said Dr. Lawrence. "Do you have the key, Walter?" he asked.

Silverman handed it to him, and the doctor opened the glass display cabinet. Quickly he made a cursory examination of either body. "This is Sethos," he stated flatly. "See, there's the wound from Greg's bullet." He pointed to a slight indentation in the brittle husk that stretched tenuously across the bones. "If I weren't afraid the whole thing would come unglued, I could probe and I bet I'd find the slug still there."

"You mentioned Sethos' spirit not being at rest, Walter," said Greg. "How about Paneb's?"

Silverman shrugged. "He's inconsequential," said the other. "In any tale of ghosts or unsettled spirits, it's never the slobs like Paneb who haunt the castle or the ancestral lands. It takes someone who displayed a keener sensitivity in life—be it for good or bad—people like Sethos and Nebnofer. No, I'd say Paneb had already been roasting for thirty-five centuries. But Sethos fought it out with Nebnofer in life, and I have a funny feeling we wouldn't have gone through what we did unless both of them were seeking release."

"Well," said Ken, "if there's any way to put the poor old guy to rest, why don't we do it? Any suggestions?" He looked about at his companions.

"You know," replied Silverman, "this idea struck

me some time back—before the four of us made the trip, actually. But now, I think several factors combined to make it happen. This is only theory, mind you, but I think…to begin with…it wasn't necessarily sex that triggered it. I think any peak of emotional reaction would have worked as well—anger, extreme fear, anything that would normally cause a strong flow of adrenalin."

"Then it wasn't the idol?" asked Ken.

"Oh, it was the idol…partially," said the anthropologist. "It was a combination of the idol and whatever powers it holds, plus the unresolved conflict between the spirits of Nebnofer and Sethos…and maybe, just a little help from Anubis."

"You're getting yourself out on a limb again," mumbled Paul Lawrence.

"Well, let's try something," said Silverman. "The mummy has never been very far from the god, even since the two of them were taken from the tomb. Neither have the skeletons, for that matter. I'd like to see what happens if we do what Nebnofer did to the other idol in the Hall of Gods."

Kicking off his shoes, Silverman climbed onto the pedestal. He reached up and wrenched one of the ruby eyes from its socket. "Sorry, old boy," he whispered. His fingers closed about the second, and he jumped back to the floor.

"I wish I could be sure before I do this," he muttered. He looked sadly at the two precious gems in his hands, admiring their brilliance for the last time. "But I think we owe this much to Nebnofer." So saying, he pulled back his arm and, with all his might, threw the two jewels against the idol's base.

Paul could not suppress a gasp as the valuable gems shattered against the black stone. Behind them, so soft it was impossible for either to be sure he really heard it, there seemed to be a sound...a brief, low moan? A stir of ancient bones? Both men turned to look at the mummy, but there was no physical evidence of any change. If it had indeed made some response, neither could define it.

But Paul walked a couple of paces toward the glass case where the skeletons were on display. "Look," he said. He pointed to the spot where Sethos' remains had been a moment before. Nothing was left but a tumbled heap of ashes. "Of course, I might have caused that when I touched it," said the doctor weakly.

"Maybe," replied Silverman doubtfully. Then he turned his gaze upon the god. "Well, I'll be damned!" he whispered.

Paul followed the line of his companion's gaze. The smile was gone! The lines about the idol's mouth seemed to maintain the same configuration; yet the over-all effect was no longer the Mona Lisa smile. Like any other graven idol from the ancient tombs, Anubis now stared before him in blank, sightless solemnity.

"Maybe it was just the rubies," suggested Paul.

"Or maybe that he isn't fooling anyone anymore," said Walter.

"More to the point," replied Paul, "how much has he fooled us?"

Walter shrugged his shoulders, and sat back on the edge of Nebnofer's sarcophagus. "I don't think we're ever going to be able to answer that with any degree of scientific...empirical certainty," he said. "Let me tell you what I think, and unless you have a better explanation, I suggest we leave it there..."

Paul nodded. "I'm listening," he said. He stood facing Walter, the toe of his shoe stirring the red, crystalline particles...all that remained of the ruby eyes.

They both regarded the collection of dust with a wistful expression. "No use crying over that," said Walter. "But it wasn't just impulse that led me to do it. I remembered Ken's remark about the first time we went. Remember, the soldiers seemed to have been expecting him? At least, they knew he had 'defiled the gods'? What he and Greg had done was somehow known, and that knowledge could only have come from Nebnofer. The High Priest must have had some glimmer of foresight, though it's obvious he never saw it clearly. Neither he nor Sethos ever fully understood the powers they possessed.

"The theory of the alien race, and the residue of an advanced technology..." added Paul Lawrence.

"Yes, either that or a carry-over from some long-dead age of wisdom—during the Old Kingdom, maybe—when whatever force it was that drove primitive men up from the level of his fellow beasts may still have been preserved. But, I prefer the alien theory," Walter admitted. "It's cleaner and fits more easily with what we know. Still, we regular mortals hold certain potentials within us that we haven't learned to use...at least not in this stage of civilization. We have machines to do the work for us. Back in the primeval past, without machines, I wonder if the human brain might not have utilized the powers we don't need, because of our overpowering technology."

"The further one goes back into history, the more accepting people seem to be of supernatural phenomena." Paul agreed. "Of course, they were also more ignorant and gullible."

"And more apt to take things at face value...not afraid to admit the existence of forces and manifestations they could not explain."

"Well..." said Paul. "I guess we'll never know. But how about the men who died while Nebnofer was trying to cleanse the second idol? Do you think we might have altered history?"

"No," replied Walter. "I think it was all in the cards when the four of us went back. Don't forget, Nebnofer's mummy and the skeletons of Paneb and Sethos were already here...in the museum. It was a cycle; a merry-go-round...and the only place we could jump on was through the god. Of course, if we did change history we wouldn't know it, would we? I mean, if things are different now from what they were before we left, the alternation would have been... retroactive. We wouldn't remember it as it was before...only as it presently exists."

As Walter finished speaking, Paul glanced around, suddenly realizing their two friends were missing. "They were here before we smashed the rubies," he said. "Christ, you don't suppose...?"

"Oh, I'm sure.... It wouldn't fit!" Walter insisted. He grabbed Paul's hand. "Come on," he said, starting to laugh. He dragged his companion out of the Egyptian room and down the corridor toward the guards' quarters.

Before they reached the door, the tell-tale twang of bedsprings told them what they'd find. "Love!" said

Paul Lawrence, shaking his head. "Love is for the very young!"

Walter stopped, his back against the wall as he pulled his friend into the tight enclosure of his arms. "That's another theory that lacks empirical proof," he whispered. His lips clung to Paul's and the doctor knew another logical assumption was about to crumple.

The Masquerade Erotic Newsletter

"Here's a very provocative, very professional [newsletter]...made up of intelligent erotic writing... Stimulating, yet not sleazy photos add to the picture and also help make this zine a high quality publication." —Gray Areas

From **Masquerade Books**, the World's Leading Publisher of Erotica, comes *The Masquerade Erotic Newsletter*—the best source for provocative, cutting-edge fiction, sizzling pictorials, scintillating and illuminating exposes of the sex industry, and probing reviews of the latest books and videos.

Featured writers and articles have included:

Lars Eighner • *Why I Write Gay Erotica*
Pat Califia • *Among Us, Against Us*
Felice Picano • *An Interview with Samuel R. Delany*
Samuel R. Delany • *The Mad Man* (excerpt)
Maxim Jakubowski • *Essex House: The Rise and Fall of Speculative Erotica*
Red Jordan Arobateau • *Reflections of a Lesbian Trick*
Aaron Travis • *Lust*
Nancy Ava Miller, M. Ed. • *Beyond Personal*
Tuppy Owens • *Female Erotica in Great Britain*
Trish Thomas • *From Dyke to Dude*
Barbara Nitke • *Resurrection*
and many more....

The newsletter has also featured stunning photo essays by such masters of fetish photography as **Robert Chouraqui, Eric Kroll, Richard Kern,** and **Trevor Watson.**

A one-year subscription (6 issues) to the *Newsletter* costs $30.00. Use the accompanying coupon to subscribe now—for an uninterrupted string of the most provocative of pleasures (as well as a special gift, offered to subscribers only!).

Free
GIFT

BADBOY

JOHN PRESTON

Tales from the Dark Lord II   **$4.95/176-4**

The second volume of acclaimed eroticist John Preston's masterful short stories. Also includes an interview with the author, and an explicit screenplay written for pornstar Scott O'Hara. An explosive collection from one of erotic publishing's most fertile imaginations.

Tales from the Dark Lord   **$5.95/323-6**

A new collection of twelve stunning works from the man *Lambda Book Report* called "the Dark Lord of gay erotica." The relentless ritual of lust and surrender is explored in all its manifestations in this heart-stopping triumph of authority and vision from the Dark Lord!

The Arena   **$4.95/3083-0**

There is a place on the edge of fantasy where every desire is indulged with abandon. Men go there to unleash beasts, to let demons roam free, to abolish all limits. At the center of each tale are the men who serve there, who offer themselves for the consummation of any passion, whose own bottomless urges compel their endless subservience.

The Heir • The King   **$4.95/3048-2**

The ground-breaking novel *The Heir*, written in the lyric voice of the ancient myths, tells the story of a world where slaves and masters create a new sexual society. This edition also includes a completely original work, *The King*, the story of a soldier who discovers his monarch's most secret desires. Available only from Badboy.

Mr. Benson   **$4.95/3041-5**

A classic erotic novel from a time when there was no limit to what a man could dream of doing.... Jamie is an aimless young man lucky enough to encounter Mr. Benson. He is soon led down the path of erotic enlightenment, learning to accept cruelty as love, anguish as affection, and this man as his master. From an opulent penthouse to the infamous Mineshaft, Jamie's incredible adventures never fail to excite—especially when the going gets rough! First serialized in *Drummer, Mr. Benson* became an immediate classic that inspired many imitators. Preston's knockout novel returns to claim the territory it mapped out years ago. The first runaway success in gay SM literature, *Mr. Benson* is sure to inspire further generations.

THE MISSION OF ALEX KANE

Sweet Dreams   **$4.95/3062-8**

It's the triumphant return of gay action hero Alex Kane! This classic series has been revised and updated especially for Badboy, and includes loads of raw action. In *Sweet Dreams*, Alex travels to Boston where he takes on a street gang that stalks gay teenagers. Mighty Alex Kane wreaks a fierce and terrible vengeance on those who prey on gay people everywhere!

Golden Years   **$4.95/3069-5**

When evil threatens the plans of a group of older gay men, Kane's got the muscle to take it head on. Along the way, he wins the support—and very specialized attentions—of a cowboy plucked right out of the Old West. But Kane and the Cowboy have a surprise waiting for them....

MR. BENSON

JOHN PRESTON

Deadly Lies
$4.95/3076-8

Politics is a dirty business and the dirt becomes deadly when a political smear campaign targets gay men. Who better to clean things up than Alex Kane! Alex comes to protect the dreams, and lives, of gay men imperiled by lies.

Stolen Moments
$4.95/3098-9

Houston's evolving gay community is victimized by a malicious newspaper editor who is more than willing to sacrifice gays on the altar of circulation. He never counted on Alex Kane, fearless defender of gay dreams and desires everywhere.

Secret Danger
$4.95/111-X

Homophobia: a pernicious social ill hardly confined by America's borders. Alex Kane and the faithful Danny are called to a small European country, where a group of gay tourists is being held hostage by ruthless terrorists. Luckily, the Mission of Alex Kane stands as firm foreign policy.

Lethal Silence
$4.95/125-X

The Mission of Alex Kane thunders to a conclusion. Chicago becomes the scene of the right-wing's most noxious plan—facilitated by unholy political alliances. Alex and Danny head to the Windy City to take up battle with the mercenaries who would squash gay men underfoot.

JAY SHAFFER

Shooters
$5.95/284-1

A new set of stories from the author of the best-selling erotic collections *Wet Dreams*, *Full Service* and *Animal Handlers*. No mere catalog of random acts, *Shooters* tells the stories of a variety of stunning men and the ways they connect in sexual and non-sexual ways. A virtuoso storyteller, Shaffer always gets his man.

Animal Handlers
$4.95/264-7

Another volume from a master of scorching fiction. In Shaffer's world, each and every man finally succumbs to the animal urges deep inside. And if there's any creature that promises a wild time, it's a beast who's been caged for far too long.

Full Service
$4.95/150-0

A baker's dirty dozen from the author of *Wet Dreams*. Wild men build up steam until they finally let loose. No-nonsense guys bear down hard on each other as they work their way toward release in this finely detailed assortment of masculine fantasies.

Wet Dreams
$4.95/142-X

These tales take a hot look at the obsessions that keep men up all night—from simple skin-on-skin to more unusual pleasures. Provocative and affecting, this is a nightful of dreams you won't forget in the morning.

D.V. SADERO

Revolt of the Naked
$4.95/261-2

In a distant galaxy, there are two classes of humans: Freemen and Nakeds. Freemen are full citizens in this system, which allows for the buying and selling of Nakeds at whim. Nakeds live only to serve their Masters, and obey every sexual order with haste and devotion. Until the day of revolution—when an army of sex toys rises in anger....

In the Alley
$4.95/144-6

Twenty cut-to-the-chase yarns inspired by the all-American male. Hardworking men—from cops to carpenters—bring their own special skills and impressive tools to the most satisfying job of all: capturing and breaking the male sexual beast. Hot, incisive and way over the top!

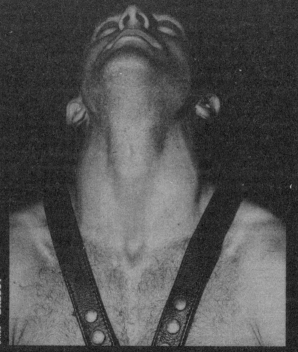

FULL
SERVICE

$4.95 · BADBOY

JAY SHAFFER

KYLE STONE

Hot Bauds $5.95/285-X
The author of *Fantasy Board* and *The Initiation of PB 500* combed cyberspace for the hottest fantasies of the world's horniest hackers. From bulletin boards called Studs, The Mine Shaft, Back Door and the like, Stone has assembled the first collection of the raunchy erotica so many gay men cruise the Information Superhighway for. Plug in—and get ready to download....

Fantasy Board $4.95/212-4
The author of the scalding sci-fi adventures of PB 500 explores the more foreseeable future—through the intertwined lives (and private parts) of a collection of randy computer hackers. On the Lambda Gate BBS, every hot and horny male is in search of a little virtual satisfaction.contented.

The Citadel $4.95/198-5
The thundering sequel to *The Initiation of PB 500*. Having proven himself worthy of his stunning master, Micah—now known only as '500'—will face new challenges and hardships after his entry into the forbidding Citadel. Only his master knows what awaits—and whether Micah will again distinguish himself as the perfect instrument of pleasure....

Rituals $4.95/168-3
Via a computer bulletin board, a young man finds himself drawn into a series of sexual rites that transform him into the willing slave of a mysterious stranger. Gradually, all vestiges of his former life are thrown off, and he learns to live for his Master's touch.... A high-tech fable of sexual surrender.

The Initiation PB 500 $4.95/141-1
He is a stranger on their planet, unschooled in their language, and ignorant of their customs. But this man, Micah—now known only by his number—will soon be trained in every last detail of erotic personal service. And, once nurtured and transformed into the perfect physical specimen, he must begin proving himself worthy of the master who has chosen him.... A scalding sci-fi epic, continued in *The Citadel*.

PHIL ANDROS

The Joy Spot $5.95/301-5
"Andros gives to the gay mind what Tom of Finland gives the gay eye—this is archetypal stuff. There's none better."

—John F. Karr, *Manifest Reader*

A classic from one of the founding fathers of gay porn. *The Joy Spot* looks at some of Andros' favorite types—cops, servicemen, truck drivers—and the sleaze they love. Nothing's too rough, and these men are always ready. So get ready to give it up—or have it taken by force!

ROBERT BAHR

Sex Show $4.95/225-6
Luscious dancing boys. Brazen, explicit acts. Unending stimulation. Take a seat, and get very comfortable, because the curtain's going up on a show no discriminating appetite can afford to miss. And the award for Best Performer...is up to you....

"BIG" BILL JACKSON

Eighth Wonder $4.95/200-0
"Big" Bill Jackson's always the randiest guy in town—no matter what town he's in. From the bright lights and back rooms of New York to the open fields and sweaty bods of a small Southern town, "Big" Bill always manages to cause a scene, and the more actors he can involve, the better! Like the man's name says, he's got more than enough for everyone, and turns nobody down....

THE
JOY
SPOT

Bayou Boy

Lars Eighner

JASON FURY

The Rope Above, the Bed Below $4.95/269-8

The irresistible Jason Fury returns—and if you thought his earlier adventures were hot, this volume will blow you away! Once again, our built, blond hero finds himself in the oddest—and most compromising—positions imaginable.

Eric's Body $4.95/151-9

Meet Jason Fury—blond, blue-eyed and up for anything. Perennial favorites in the gay press, Fury's sexiest tales are collected in book form for the first time. Ranging from the bittersweet to the surreal, these stories follow the irresistible Jason through sexual adventures unlike any you have ever read....

JOHN ROWBERRY

Lewd Conduct $4.95/3091-1

Flesh-and-blood men vie for power, pleasure and surrender in each of these feverish stories, and no one walks away from his steamy encounter unsated. Rowberry's men are unafraid to push the limits of civilized behavior in search of the elusive and empowering conquest.

LARS EIGHNER

Whispered in the Dark $5.95/286-8

Lars Eighner continues to produce gay fiction whose quality rivals the best in the genre. *Whispered in the Dark* continues to demonstrate Eighner's unique combination of strengths: poetic descriptive power, an unfailing ear for dialogue, and a finely tuned feeling for the nuances of male passion. *Whispered in the Dark* reasserts Eighner's claim to mastery of the gay erotica genre.

American Prelude $4.95/170-5

Another volume of irresistible Eighner tales. Praised by *The New York Times*, Eighner is widely recognized as one of our best, most exciting gay writers. What the *Times* won't admit, however, is that he is also one of gay erotica's true masters—and *American Prelude* shows why.

Bayou Boy $4.95/3084-9

Another collection of well-tuned stories from one of our finest writers. Witty and incisive, each tale explores the many ways men work up a sweat in the steamy Southwest. *Bayou Boy* also includes the "Houston Streets" stories—sexy, touching tales of growing up gay in a fast-changing world. Street smart and razor sharp—and guaranteed to warm the coldest night!

B.M.O.C. $4.95/3077-6

In a college town known as "the Athens of the Southwest," studs of every stripe are up all night—studying, naturally. In *B.M.O.C.*, Lars Eighner includes the very best of his short stories, sure to appeal to the collegian in every man. Relive university life the way it was *supposed* to be, with a cast of handsome honor students majoring in Human Homosexuality.

CALDWELL/EIGHNER

QSFx2 $5.95/278-7

One volume of the wickedest, wildest, other-worldliest yarns from two master storytellers—Clay Caldwell and Lars Eighner, the highly-acclaimed author of *Travels With Lizbeth*. Both eroticists take a trip to the furthest reaches of the sexual imagination, sending back ten stories proving that as much as things change, one thing will always remain the same....

$4.95 · **BADBOY**

AARON TRAVIS
EXPOSED

AARON TRAVIS

In the Blood $5.95/283-3

Written when Travis had just begun to explore the true power of the erotic imagination, these stories laid the groundwork for later masterpieces. Among the many rewarding rarities included in this volume: "In the Blood"—a heart-pounding descent into sexual vampirism, written with the furious erotic power that has distinguished Travis' work from the beginning.

The Flesh Fables $4.95/243-4

One of Travis' best collections, finally rereleased. *The Flesh Fables* includes "Blue Light," his most famous story, as well as other masterpieces that established him as the erotic writer to watch. And watch carefully, because Travis always buries a surprise somewhere beneath his scorching detail....

Slaves of the Empire $4.95/3054-7

The return of an undisputed classic from this master of the erotic genre.

"*Slaves of the Empire* is a wonderful mythic tale. Set against the backdrop of the exotic and powerful Roman Empire, this wonderfully written novel explores the timeless questions of light and dark in male sexuality. Travis has shown himself expert in manipulating the most primal themes and images. The locale may be the ancient world, but these are the slaves and masters of our time...."

—John Preston

Big Shots $4.95/112-8

Two fierce tales in one electrifying volume. In *Beirut,* Travis tells the story of ultimate military power and erotic subjugation; *Kip,* Travis' hypersexed and sinister take on *film noir,* appears in unexpurgated form for the first time—including the final, overwhelming chapter. Unforgettable acts and relentless passions dominate these chronicles of unimaginable lust—as seen from the points of view of raging, powerful men, and the bottomless submissives who yield to their desires. One of our rawest, most unrelenting titles.

Exposed $4.95/126-8

A volume of shorter Travis tales, each providing a unique glimpse of the horny gay male in his natural environment! Cops, college jocks, ancient Romans—even Sherlock Holmes and his loyal Watson—cruise these pages, fresh from the throbbing pen of one of our hottest authors.

Beast of Burden $4.95/105-5

Five ferocious tales from a master of lascivious prose. Innocents surrender to the brutal sexual mastery of their superiors, as taboos are shattered and replaced with the unwritten rules of masculine conquest. Intense, extreme—and totally Travis.

CLAY CALDWELL

Service, Stud $5.95/336-8

From the author of the sexy sci-fi epic *All-Stud*, comes another look at the gay future. The setting is the Los Angeles of a distant future. Here the all-male populace is divided between the served and the servants—an arrangement guaranteeing the erotic satisfaction of all involved. Until, of course, one pugnacious young stud challenges authority, and the sexual rules it so rigidly enforces....

Stud Shorts $5.95/320-1

"If anything, Caldwell's charm is more powerful, his nostalgia more poignant, the horniness he captures more sweetly, achingly acute than ever."

—Aaron Travis

A new collection of this legendary writer's latest sex-fiction. With his customary candor, Caldwell tells all about cops, cadets, truckers, farmboys (and many more) in these dirty jewels.

ALL-STUD

$4.95 (CANADA $5.95) • **BADBOY**

CLAY CALDWELL

Tailpipe Trucker $5.95/296-5

With *Tailpipe Trucker*, Clay Caldwell set the cornerstone of "trucker porn"—a story revolving around the age-old fantasy of horny men on the road. In prose as free and unvarnished as a cross-country highway, Caldwell tells the truth about Trag and Curly—two men hot for the feeling of sweaty manflesh.

Queers Like Us $4.95/262-0

"This is Caldwell at his most charming." —Aaron Travis

For years the name Clay Caldwell has been synonymous with the hottest, most finely crafted gay tales available. *Queers Like Us* is one of his best: the story of a randy mailman's trek through a landscape of willing, available studs.

All-Stud $4.95/104-7

An incredible, erotic trip into the gay future. This classic, sex-soaked tale takes place under the watchful eye of Number Ten: an omniscient figure who has decreed unabashed promiscuity as the law of his all-male land. Men exist to serve men, and all surrender to state-sanctioned fleshly indulgence.

HODDY ALLEN

Al $5.95/302-3

Al is a remarkable young man. With his long brown hair, bright green eyes and eagerness to please, many would consider him the perfect submissive. Many would like to mark him as their own—but it is at that point that Al stops. One day Al relates the entire astounding tale of his life....

1 800 906-HUNK

Hardcore phone action for *real* men. A scorching assembly of studs is waiting for your call—and eager to give you the head-trip of your life! Totally live, guaranteed one-on-one encounters. (Must be over 18.) No credit card needed. $3.98 per minute.

KEY LINCOLN

Submission Holds $4.95/266-3

A bright young talent unleashes his first collection of gay erotica. From tough to tender, the men between these covers stop at nothing to get what they want. These sweat-soaked tales show just how bad boys can really get....

TOM BACCHUS

Rahm $5.95/315-5

A volume spanning the many ages of hardcore queer lust—from Creation to the modern day. The imagination of Tom Bacchus brings to life an extraordinary assortment of characters, from the Father of Us All to the cowpoke next door, the early gay literati to rude, queercore mosh rats. No one is better than Bacchus at staking out sexual territory with a swagger and a sly grin.

Bone $4.95/177-2

Queer musings from the pen of one of today's hottest young talents. A fresh outlook on fleshly indulgence yields more than a few pleasant surprises. Horny Tom Bacchus maps out the tricking ground of a new generation.

VINCE GILMAN

The Slave Prince $4.95/199-3

"...I was never a slave, Pasha thought, smiling proudly to himself. I used to hold orgies with the men from my father's honor guard, late at night, when my father was busy with his harem boys and knew no better...."

A runaway royal learns the true meaning of power when he comes under the hand of Korat—a man well-versed in the many ways of subjugating a young man to his relentless sexual appetite.

$4.95 • BADBOY

BONE

TOM BACCHUS

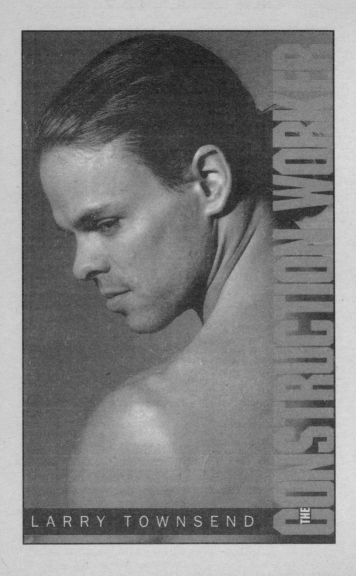

THE CONSTRUCTION WORKER

LARRY TOWNSEND

BOB VICKERY

Skin Deep $4.95/265-5

Talk about "something for everyone!" *Skin Deep* contains so many varied beauties no one will go away unsatisfied. No tantalizing morsel of manflesh is overlooked—or left unexplored! Beauty may be only skin deep, but a handful of beautiful skin is a tempting proposition.

JAMES MEDLEY

Huck and Billy $4.95/245-0

Young love is always the sweetest, always the most sorrowful. Young lust, on the other hand, knows no bounds—and is often the hottest of one's life! Huck and Billy explore the desires that course through their young male bodies, determined to plumb the lusty depths of passion. Sweet and hot. Very hot.

LARRY TOWNSEND

Beware the God Who Smiles $5.95/321-X

A torrid time-travel tale from one of gay erotica's most notorious writers. Two lusty young Americans are transported to ancient Egypt—where they are embroiled in regional warfare and taken as slaves by marauding barbarians. The key to escape from this brutal bondage lies in their own rampant libidos, and urges as old as time itself.

The Construction Worker $5.95/298-1

A young, hung construction worker is sent to a building project in Central America, where he is shocked to find some ancient and unusual traditions in practice. In this isolated location, man-to-man sex is the accepted norm. The young stud quickly fits right in (and quite snugly)—until he senses that beneath the constant sexual shenanigans there moves an almost supernatural force. Soon, nothing is what it seems....

2069 Trilogy (This one-volume collection only $6.95) 244-2

For the first time, Larry Townsend's early science-fiction trilogy appears in one volume! Set in a future world, the *2069 Trilogy* includes the tight plotting and shameless male sexual pleasure that established him as one of gay erotica's first masters. This special one-volume edition available only from Badboy.

Mind Master $4.95/209-4

Who better to explore the territory of erotic dominance and submission than an author who helped define the genre—and knows that ultimate mastery always transcends the physical.

The Long Leather Cord $4.95/201-9

Chuck's stepfather is an enigma: never lacking in money or clandestine male visitors with whom he enacts intense sexual rituals. As Chuck comes to terms with his own savage desires, he begins to unravel his stepfather's mystery.

Man Sword $4.95/188-8

The *tres gai* tale of France's King Henri III. Unimaginably spoiled by his mother—the infamous Catherine de Medici—Henri is groomed from a young age to assume the throne of France. Along the way, he encounters enough sexual schemers and randy politicos to alter one's picture of history forever!

The Faustus Contract $4.95/167-5

Two attractive young men desperately need $1000. Will do anything. Travel OK. Danger OK. Call anytime... Two cocky young hustlers get more than they bargained for in this story of lust and its discontents.

The Gay Adventures of Captain Goose $4.95/169-1

The hot and tender young Jerome Gander is sentenced to serve aboard the *H.M.S. Faerigold*—a ship manned by the most hardened, unrepentant criminals. In no time, Gander becomes well-versed in the ways of men at sea, and the *Faerigold* becomes the most notorious ship of its day.

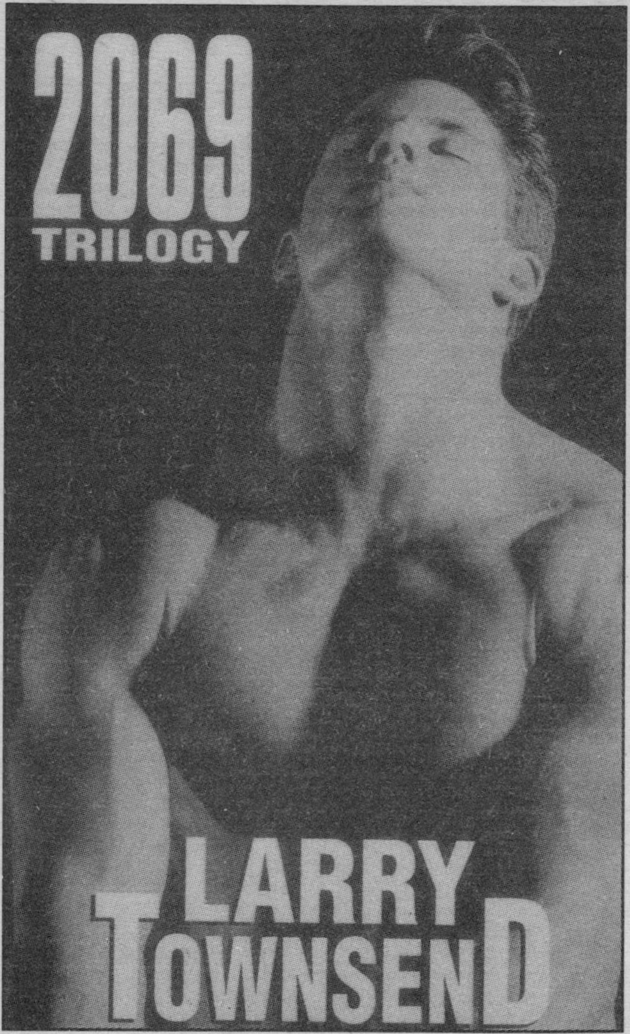

2069
TRILOGY
LARRY
TOWNSEND

Chains $4.95/158-6

Picking up street punks has always been risky, but in Larry Townsend's classic *Chains*, it sets off a string of events that must be read to be believed. One of Townsend's most remarkable works, *Chains* explores the dynamics of the male sexual bond—and what happens when a weak link finally gives....

Kiss of Leather $4.95/161-6

Acclaimed gay porn pioneer Larry Townsend's first leather title. A look at the acts and attitudes of an earlier generation of leathermen, *Kiss of Leather* is full to bursting with the gritty, raw action that has distinguished Townsend's work for years. Pain and pleasure mix in this tightly-plotted tale.

Run No More $4.95/152-7

The continuation of Larry Townsend's legendary *Run, Little Leather Boy*. This volume follows the further adventures of Townsend's leatherclad narrator as he travels every sexual byway available to the S/M male. As he works his way toward elite circles, Wayne begins to make shocking discoveries....

Run, Little Leather Boy $4.95/143-8

The classic story of one young man's sexual awakening. A chronic underachiever, Wayne seems to be going nowhere fast. When his father puts him to work for a living, Wayne soon finds himself bored with the everyday—and increasingly drawn to the masculine intensity of a dark sexual underground....

The Scorpius Equation $4.95/119-5

A sex-packed science fiction adventure from the fertile imagination of Larry Townsend. Set in the far future, *The Scorpius Equation* is the story of a man caught between the demands of two galactic empires. Our randy hero must match wits—and more—with the incredible forces that rule his world.

The Sexual Adventures of Sherlock Holmes $4.95/3097-0

Holmes' most satisfying adventures, from the unexpurgated memoirs of the faithful Mr. Watson. "A Study in Scarlet" is transformed to expose Mrs. Hudson as a man in drag, the Diogenes Club as an S/M arena, and clues only Sherlock Holmes could piece together. A baffling tale of sex and mystery.

DEREK ADAMS

My Double Life $5.95/314-7

Every man leads a double life, dividing his hours between the mundanities of the day and the outrageous pursuits of the night. In this, his second collection of stories, the author of *Boy Toy* and creator of sexy P.I. Miles Diamond shines a little light on what men do when no one's looking. Derek Adams proves, once again, that he's the ultimate chronicler of our wicked ways.

Boy Toy $4.95/260-4

Poor Brendan Callan—sent to the Brentwood Academy against his will, he soon finds himself the guinea pig of a crazed geneticist. Brendan becomes irresistibly alluring—a talent designed for endless pleasure, but coveted by others for the most unsavory means....

Heat Wave $4.95/159-4

"His body was draped in baggy clothes, but there was hardly any doubt that they covered anything less than perfection.... His slacks were cinched tight around a narrow waist, and the rise of flesh pushing against the thin fabric promised a firm, melon-shaped ass.... The little flame of lust that had been tickling in my belly flared into a full-scale conflagration..."

Miles Diamond and the Demon of Death $4.95/251-5

Derek Adams' gay gumshoe Miles Diamond returns for further adventures of the good old-fashioned private eye variety. Miles always seems to find himself in the stickiest situations—with any stud whose path he crosses! His adventures with "The Demon of Death" promise another carnal carnival.

The Adventures of Miles Diamond $4.95/118-7

The hot adventures of horny P.I. Miles Diamond. "The Case of the Missing Twin" promises to be a most rewarding case, packed as it is with randy studs. Miles sets about uncovering all as he tracks down the elusive and delectable Daniel Travis.... The volume that made Miles Diamond a sensation.

KELVIN BELIELE
If the Shoe Fits $4.95/223-X

An essential and winning volume of tales exploring a world where randy boys can't help but do what comes naturally—as often as possible! Sweaty male bodies grapple in pleasure, proving the old adage: if the shoe fits, one might as well slip right in....

VICTOR TERRY
WHiPs $4.95/254-X

Connoisseurs of gay writing have known Victor Terry's work for some time. With *WHiPs*, Terry joins BADBOY's roster at last with this punishing collection of short stories. Cruising for a hot man? You'd better be, because one way or another, these WHiPs—officers of the Wyoming Highway Patrol—are gonna pull you over for a little impromptu interrogation....

MAX EXANDER
Deeds of the Night: Tales of Eros and Passion $5.95/348-1

MAXimum porn! Exander's a writer who's seen it all—and is more than happy to describe every inch of it in pulsating detail. From the man behind *Mansex* and *Leathersex*—two whirlwind tours of the hypermasculine libido—comes another unrestrained volume of sweat-soaked fantasies.

Leathersex $4.95/210-8

Another volume of hard-hitting tales from merciless Max Exander. This time he focuses on the leatherclad lust that draws together only the most willing and talented of tops and bottoms—for an all-out orgy of limitless surrender and control....

Mansex $4.95/160-8

"Tex was all his name implied: tall, lanky but muscular, with reddish-blond hair and a handsome, chiseled face that was somewhat leathered. Mark was the classic leatherman: a huge, dark stud in chaps, with a big black moustache, hairy chest and enormous muscles. Exactly the kind of men Todd liked—strong, hunky, masculine, ready to take control...." Rough sex for rugged men.

TOM CAFFREY
Hitting Home $4.95/222-1

One of our newest Badboys weighs in with a scorching collection of stories. Titillating and compelling, the stories in *Hitting Home* make a strong case for there being only one thing on a man's mind.

TORSTEN BARRING
Prisoners of Torquemada $5.95/252-3

The infamously unsparing Torsten Barring (*The Switch, Peter Thornwell, Shadowman*) weighs in with another volume sure to push you over the edge. How cruel is the "therapy" practiced at Casa Torquemada? Rest assured that Barring is just the writer to evoke such steamy malevolence.

Shadowman $4.95/178-0

From spoiled Southern aristocrats to randy youths sowing wild oats at the local picture show, Barring's imagination works overtime in these vignettes of homolust—past, present and future.

Peter Thornwell $4.95/149-7

Follow the exploits of Peter Thornwell as he goes from misspent youth to scandalous stardom, all thanks to an insatiable libido and love for the lash. Peter and his sex-crazed sidekicks find themselves pursued by merciless men from all walks of life in this torrid take on Horatio Alger.

SLOW
BURN

$4.95 (CANADA $5.95) · BADBOY

ANONYMOUS

The Switch $4.95/3061-X

Sometimes a man needs a good whipping, and *The Switch* certainly makes a case! Laced with images of men "in too-tight Levi's, with the faces of angels... and the bodies of devils." Packed with hot studs and unrelenting passions.

S O N N Y   F O R D

Reunion in Florence $4.95/3070-9

Captured by Turks, Adrian and Tristan will do anything to save their heads. When Tristan is threatened by a Sultan's jealousy, Adrian begins his quest for the only man alive who can replace Tristan as the object of the Sultan's lust. The two soon learn to rely on their wild sexual imaginations.

R O G E R   H A R M A N

First Person $4.95/179-9

A highly personal collection. Each story here takes the form of an uncensored confessional—told by men who've got plenty to confess! From the "first time ever" to firsts of different kinds, *First Person* tells truths too hot to be fiction.

C H R I S T O P H E R   M O R G A N

Muscle Bound $4.95/3028-8

In the New York City bodybuilding scene, country boy Tommy joins forces with sexy Will Rodriguez in a battle of wits and biceps at the hottest gym in the Village, where the weak are bound and crushed by iron-pumping gods. Muscle-studs run amuck!

S E A N   M A R T I N

Scrapbook $4.95/224-8

Imagine a book filled with only the best, most vivid remembrances...a book brimming with every hot, sexy encounter its pages can hold... Now you need only open up *Scrapbook* to know that such a volume really exists....

C A R O   S O L E S   &   S T A N   T A L

Bizarre Dreams $4.95/187-X

An anthology of stirring voices dedicated to exploring the dark side of human fantasy. Including such BADBOY favorites as John Preston, Lars Eighner and Kyle Stone, *Bizarre Dreams* brings together the most talented practitioners of "dark fantasy": the most forbidden sexual realm of all.

J . A .   G U E R R A

BADBOY Fantasies $4.95/3049-0

When love eludes them—lust will do! Thrill-seeking men caught up in vivid dreams and dark mysteries—these are the brief encounters you'll pant and gasp over in *Badboy Fantasies*.

Slow Burn $4.95/3042-3

Welcome to the Body Shoppe, where men's lives cross in the pursuit of muscle. Torsos get lean and hard, pecs widen, and stomachs ripple in these sexy stories of the power and perils of physical perfection.

Men at Work $4.95/3027-X

He's the most gorgeous man you have ever seen. You yearn for his touch at night in your empty bed; but he's your co-worker! A collection of eight sizzling stories of man-to-man on-the-job training.

D A V E   K I N N I C K

Sorry I Asked $4.95/3090-3

Unexpurgated interviews with gay porn's rank and file. Dave Kinnick, long-time video reviewer for *Advocate Men*, gets personal with the men behind (and under) the "stars," and reveals the dirt and details of the porn business.

MICHAEL LOWENTHAL, ED.

The BADBOY Erotic Library Volume I   **$4.95/190-X**

A Secret Life, Imre, Sins of the Cities of the Plain, Teleny and more—the hottest sections of these perennial favorites come together for the first time.

The BADBOY Erotic Library Volume II   **$4.95/211-6**

This time, selections are taken from *Mike and Me* and *Muscle Bound, Men at Work, Badboy Fantasies,* and *Slowburn.*

ANONYMOUS

A Secret Life   **$4.95/3017-2**

Meet Master Charles: only eighteen, and *quite* innocent, until his arrival at the Sir Percival's Royal Academy, where the daily lessons are supplemented with a crash course in pure, sweet sexual heat!

Sins of the Cities of the Plain   **$5.95/322-8**

Indulge yourself in the scorching memoirs of young man-about-town Jack Saul. From his earliest erotic moments with Jerry in the dark of his bedchamber, to his shocking dalliances with the lords and "ladies" of British high society, Jack's positively *sinful* escapades grow wilder with every chapter!

Imre   **$4.95/3019-9**

What dark secrets, what fiery passions lay hidden behind strikingly beautiful Lieutenant Imre's emerald eyes? An extraordinary lost classic of fantasy, obsession, gay erotic desire, and romance in a tiny town on the eve of WWI.

Teleny   **$4.95/3020-2**

A dark Victorian classic, often attributed to Oscar Wilde. A young stud of independent means seeks only a succession of voluptuous and forbidden pleasures, but instead finds love and tragedy when he becomes embroiled in a mysterious cult devoted to fulfilling only the very darkest of fantasies.

Mike and Me   **$4.95/3035-0**

Mike joined the gym squad to bulk up on muscle. Little did he know he'd be turning on every sexy muscle jock in Minnesota! Hard bodies collide in a series of workouts designed to generate a whole lot more than rips and cuts.

PAT CALIFIA

The Sexpert   **$4.95/3034-2**

For many years now, the sophisticated gay man has known that he can turn to one authority for answers to virtually any question on the subjects of intimacy and sexual performance. Straight from the pages of *Advocate Men* comes The Sexpert! From penis size to toy care, bar behavior to AIDS awareness, The Sexpert responds to real concerns with uncanny wisdom and a razor wit.

FOR A FREE COPY OF THE COMPLETE MASQUERADE CATALOG,
MAIL THIS COUPON TO:
MASQUERADE BOOKS/DEPT X74K
801 SECOND AVENUE, NEW YORK, NY 10017
OR FAX TO 212 986-7355
All transactions are strictly confidential and we never sell, give or trade any customer's name.

NAME _____

ADDRESS _____

CITY _____ STATE _____ ZIP _____

HARD CANDY

RED JORDAN AROBATEAU

Dirty Pictures   **$6.95/345-7**

Another red-hot tale from lesbian sensation Red Jordan Arobateau. *Dirty Pictures* tells the story of a lonely butch tending bar—and the femme she finally calls her own. With the same precision that made *Lucy and Mickey* a breakout debut, Arobateau tells a love story that's the flip-side of "lesbian chic." Not to be missed.

Praise for Arobateau's *Lucy and Mickey*:
"Both deeply philosophical and powerfully erotic.... A necessary reminder to all who blissfully—some may say ignorantly—ride the wave of lesbian chic into the mainstream."

—Heather Findlay, editor-in-chief of *Girlfriends*

LARS EIGHNER

Gay Cosmos   **$6.95/236-1**

A thought-provoking volume from widely acclaimed author Lars Eighner. Eighner has distinguished himself as not only one of America's most accomplished new voices, but a solid-seller—his erotic titles alone have become bestsellers and classics of the genre. Eighner describes *Gay Cosmos* as being a volume of "essays on the place, meaning, and purpose of homosexuality in the Universe, and gay sexuality on human societies."

JAMES COLTON

Todd   **$6.95/312-0**

A remarkably frank novel from an earlier age. With *Todd*, Colton took on the complexities of American race relations, becoming one of the first writers to explore interracial love between two men. Set in 1971, Colton's novel examines the relationship of Todd and Felix, and the ways in which it is threatened by not only the era's politics, but the timeless stumbling block called "the reappearing former lover." Tender and uncompromising, *Todd* takes on issues the gay community struggles with to this day.

The Outward Side   **$6.95/304-X**

The return of a classic tale of one man's struggle with his deepest needs. Marc Lingard, a handsome, respected young minister, finds himself at a crossroads. The homophobic persecution of a local resident unearths Marc's long-repressed memories of a youthful love affair, and he is irrepressibly drawn to his forbidden urges. Originally published two years after Stonewall, Colton's novel helped pave the way for popular gay literature in America. *The Outward Side* promises to enthrall a new generation of gay readers.

STAN LEVENTHAL

Skydiving on Christopher Street   **$6.95/287-6**

"Generosity, evenness, fairness to the reader, sensitivity—these are qualities that most contemporary writers take for granted or overrule with stylistics. In Leventhal's writing they not only stand out, they're positively addictive." —Dennis Cooper

Aside from a hateful job, a hateful apartment, a hateful world and an increasingly hateful lover, life seems, well, all right for the protagonist of Stan Leventhal's latest novel, *Skydiving on Christopher Street*. Having already lost most of his friends to AIDS, how could things get any worse? But things soon do, and he's forced to endure much more before finding a new strength amidst his memories.

FELICE PICANO

Men Who Loved Me   **$6.95/274-4**

In 1966, at the tender-but-bored age of twenty-two, Felice Picano abandoned New York, determined to find true love in Europe. Almost immediately, he encounters Djanko—an exquisite prodigal who sweeps Felice off his feet with the endless string of extravagant parties, glamorous clubs and glittering premieres that made up Rome's *dolce vita*. When the older (slightly) and wiser (vastly) Picano returns to New York at last, he plunges into the city's thriving gay community—experiencing the frenzy and heartbreak that came to define Greenwich Village society in the 1970s. Lush and warm, *Men Who Loved Me* is a matchless portrait of an unforgettable decade.

"Zesty... spiked with adventure and romance.... a distinguished and humorous portrait of a vanished age."   *—Publishers Weekly*

"A stunner... captures the free-wheeling spirit of an era."
                                                         —The Advocate

"Rich, engaging, engrossing... a ravishingly exotic romance."
                                                        —New York Native

Ambi*dextrous*   **$6.95/275-2**

"Deftly evokes those placid Eisenhower years of bicycles, boners, and book reports. Makes us remember what it feels like to be a child..."
                                                         —The Advocate

"Compelling and engrossing... will conjure up memories of everyone's adolescence, straight or gay."   *—Out!*

The touching and funny memories of childhood—as only Felice Picano could tell them. Ambi*dextrous* tells the story of Picano's youth in the suburbs of New York during the '50s. Beginning at age eleven, Picano's "memoir in the form of a novel" tells all: home life, school face-offs, the ingenuous sophistications of his first sexual steps. In three years' time, he's had his first gay fling—and is on his way to becoming the writer about whom the *L.A. Herald Examiner* said "[he] can run the length of experience from the lyrical to the lewd without missing a beat." A moving memoir, **Ambi*dextrous*** is sure to reawaken the child's sense of wonder inside everyone.

WILLIAM TALSMAN

The Gaudy Image   **$6.95/263-9**

Unavailable for years, William Talsman's remarkable pre-Stonewall gay novel returns. Filled with insight into gay life of an earlier period, *The Gaudy Image* stands poised to take its place alongside *Better Angel*, *Quatrefoil* and *The City and the Pillar* as not only an invaluable piece of the community's literary history, but a fascinating, highly-entertaining reading experience.

"To read *The Gaudy Image* now is not simply to enjoy a great novel or an artifact of gay history, it is to see first-hand the very issues of identity and positionality with which gay men and gay culture were struggling in the decades before Stonewall. For what Talsman is dealing with...is the very question of how we conceive ourselves gay."
                                —from the Introduction by Michael Bronski

A RICHARD KASAK BOOK

MICHAEL ROWE

WRITING BELOW THE BELT: Conversations with Erotic Authors

Award-winning journalist Michael Rowe interviewed the best and brightest erotic writers—both those well-known for their work in the field and those just starting out—and presents the collected wisdom in *Writing Below the Belt*. Rowe speaks frankly with cult favorites such as Pat Califia, crossover success stories like John Preston, and up-and-comers Michael Lowenthal and Will Leber. In each revealing conversation, the personal, the political and the just plain prurient collide and complement one another in fascinating ways.

$19.95/363-5

RANDY TUROFF, EDITOR

LESBIAN WORDS: State of the Art

Lesbian Words collects one of the widest assortments of lesbian nonfiction writing in one revealing volume. Dorothy Allison, Jewelle Gomez, Judy Grahn, Eileen Myles, Robin Podolsky and many others are represented by some of their best work, looking at not only the current fashionability the media has brought to the lesbian "image," but important considerations of the lesbian past via historical inquiry and personal recollections. A fascinating, provocative volume, *Lesbian Words* is a virtual primer to contemporary trends in lesbian thought.

$10.95/340-6

EURYDICE

f/32

f/32 has been called "the most controversial and dangerous novel ever written by a woman." With the story of Ela (whose name is a pseudonym for orgasm), Eurydice won the National Fiction competition sponsored by Fiction Collective Two and Illinois State University. A funny, disturbing quest for unity, *f/32* prompted Frederic Tuten to proclaim that "almost any page... redeems us from the anemic writing and banalities we have endured in the past decade of bloodless fiction."

$10.95/350-3

LARRY TOWNSEND

ASK LARRY

Twelve years of Masterful advice from Larry Townsend, the leatherman's long-time confidant and adviser. Starting just before the onslaught of AIDS, Townsend wrote the "Leather Notebook" column for *Drummer* magazine. Now, with *Ask Larry*, readers can avail themselves of Townsend's collected wisdom and contemporary commentary—a careful consideration of the way life has changed in the AIDS era, and the specific ways in which the disease has altered perceptions of once-simple problems.

$12.95/289-2

WILLIAM CARNEY

THE REAL THING

"Carney gives us a good look at the mores and lifestyle of the first generation of gay leathermen. A chilling mystery/romance novel as well."
—Pat Califia

With a new Introduction by Michael Bronski. William Carney's *The Real Thing* has long served as a touchstone in any consideration of gay "edge fiction." First published in 1968, this uncompromising story of New York leathermen received instant acclaim—and in the years since, has become a rare and highly-prized volume to those lucky enough to acquire a copy. Finally, *The Real Thing* returns from exile, ready to thrill a new generation—and reacquaint itself with its original audience.

$10.95/280-9

LOOKING FOR MR. PRESTON

Edited by Laura Antoniou, *Looking for Mr. Preston* includes work by Lars Eighner, Pat Califia, Michael Bronski, Felice Picano, Joan Nestle, Larry Townsend, Andrew Holleran, Michael Lowenthal, and others who contributed interviews, essays and personal reminiscences of John Preston—a man whose career spanned the industry from the early pages of the *Advocate* to national bestseller lists. Preston was the author of over twenty books, including *Franny, the Queen of Provincetown*, and *Mr. Benson*. He also edited the noted *Flesh and the Word* erotic anthologies, *Hometowns*, and *A Member of the Family*. More importantly, Preston became an inspiration, friend and occasionally a mentor to many of today's gay and lesbian authors and editors. Ten percent of the proceeds from sale of the book will go to the AIDS Project of Southern Maine, for whom Preston had served as President of the Board.   **$23.95/288-4**

MICHAEL LASSELL

THE HARD WAY

Lassell is a master of the necessary word. In an age of tepid and whining verse, his bawdy and bittersweet songs are like a plunge in cold champagne.

—Paul Monette

Widely anthologized and a staple of gay literary and entertainment publications nationwide, Lassell is regarded as one of the most distinctive and accomplished talents of his generation. As much a chronicle of post-Stonewall gay life as a compendium of a remarkable writer's work, *The Hard Way* is sure to appeal to anyone interested in the state of contemporary writing.   **$12.95/231-0**

JOHN PRESTON

MY LIFE AS A PORNOGRAPHER

...essential and enlightening...His sex-positive stand on safer-sex education as the only truly effective AIDS-prevention strategy will certainly not win him any conservative converts, but AIDS activists will be shouting their assent....[My Life as a Pornographer] is a bridge from the sexually liberated 1970s to the more cautious 1990s, and Preston has walked much of that way as a standard-bearer to the cause for equal rights.... —Library Journal
$12.95/135-7

HUSTLING:
A Gentleman's Guide to the Fine Art of Homosexual Prostitution

...valuable insights to many aspects of the world of gay-male prostitution. Throughout the book, Preston uses materials gathered from interviews and letters from former and active hustlers, as well as insights gleaned from his own experience as a hustler.... Preston does fulfill his desire to entertain as well as educate. —Lambda Book Report
...fun and highly literary. what more could you expect from such an accomplished activist, author and editor? —Drummer
$12.95/137-3

RUSS KICK

OUTPOSTS:
A Catalog of Rare and Disturbing Alternative Information

A huge, authoritative guide to some of the most offbeat and bizarre publications available today! Russ Kick has tracked down the real McCoy and compiled over five hundred reviews of work penned by political extremists, conspiracy theorists, hallucinogenic pathfinders, sexual explorers, religious iconoclasts and social malcontents. Better yet, each review is followed by ordering information for the many readers sure to want these publications for themselves. No one with a "need to know" can afford to miss this ultra-alternative resource.   **$18.95/0202-8**

SENSUOUS MAGIC

A G**UIDE** **FOR** A**DVENTUROUS** C**OUPLES**

SAMUEL R. DELANY
THE MAD MAN

The latest novel from Hugo- and Nebula-winning science fiction writer and critic Delany...reads like a pornographic reflection of Peter Ackroyd's Chatterton *or A.S. Byatt's* Possession*.... The pornographic element... becomes more than simple shock or titillation, though, as Delany develops an insightful dichotomy between [his protagonist]'s two worlds: the one of cerebral philosophy and dry academia, the other of heedless, 'impersonal' obsessive sexual extremism. When these worlds finally collide...the novel achieves a surprisingly satisfying resolution....*
—Publishers Weekly
$23.95/193-4

THE MOTION OF LIGHT IN WATER

The first unexpurgated American edition of award-winning author Samuel R. Delany's autobiography covers the early years of one of science fiction's most important voices. Delany paints a compelling picture of New York's East Village in the early '60s—when Bob Dylan took second billing to a certain guitar-toting science fiction writer, W. H. Auden stopped by for dinner, and a walk on the Brooklyn Bridge changed the course of a literary genre. **$12.95/133-0**

ROBERT PATRICK
TEMPLE SLAVE

...you must read this book. It draws such a tragic, and, in a way, noble portrait of Mr. Buono: It leads the reader, almost against his will, into a deep sympathy with this strange man who tried to comfort, to encourage and to feed both the worthy and the worthless... It is impossible not to mourn for this man—impossible not to praise this book. —Quentin Crisp **$12.95/191-8**

LARS EIGHNER
ELEMENTS OF AROUSAL

Critically acclaimed gay writer Lars Eighner—whose *Travels with Lizbeth* was chosen by the *New York Times Book Review* as one of the year's notable titles—develops a guideline for success with one of publishing's best kept secrets: the novice-friendly field of gay erotic writing. In *Elements of Arousal*, Eighner details his craft, providing the reader with sure advice. Eighner's overview of the gay erotic market paints a picture of a diverse array of outlets for a writer's work. Because, after all, writing is what *Elements of Arousal* is about: the application and honing of the writer's craft, which brought Lars Eighner fame with not only the steamy *Bayou Boy*, but the profoundly illuminating *Travels with Lizbeth*. **$12.95/230-2**

PAT CALIFIA
SENSUOUS MAGIC

Clear, succinct and engaging even for the reader for whom S/M isn't the sexual behavior of choice.... Califia's prose is soothing, informative and non-judgmental—she both instructs her reader and explores the territory for them.... Califia is the Dr. Ruth of the alternative sexuality set....
—Lambda Book Report

Renowned erotic pioneer Pat Califia provides this honest, unpretentious peek behind the mask of dominant/submissive sexuality—an adventurous adult world of pleasure too often obscured by ignorance and fear. With her trademark wit and insight, Califia demystifies "the scene" for the novice, explaining the terminology and technique behind many misunderstood sexual practices. The adventurous (or just plain curious) lover won't want to miss this ultimate "how to" volume. One of the best-selling erotic manuals available today. **$12.95/131-4**

CARO SOLES, EDITOR

MELTDOWN!
An Anthology of Erotic Science Fiction and Dark Fantasy for Gay Men

Editor Caro Soles has put together one of the most explosive, mind-bending collections of gay erotic writing ever published. Soles illustrates the sub-genre with a quick overview of *Meltdown*'s contents:

... From the bleak futuristic world of 'meta-AIDS' where unprotected sex is against the law, to the old fashioned romance of a ghost story; from a transsexual zombie lover, to the alien hermaphrodite dancer with a secret taste for S/M, this collection covers a lot of territory that is not the usual domain of stories that explore gay sexuality. Here men pursue their tricks and lovers and dream partners through time, space and memory; from the Crusades into the distant future and on to other worlds.... **$12.95/203-5**

MASQUERADE BOOKS

TINY ALICE

The Geek   **$5.95/341-4**

A notorious cult classic. *The Geek* is told from the point of view of, well, a chicken who reports on the various perversities he witnesses as part of a traveling carnival. When a gang of renegade lesbians kidnaps Chicken and his geek, all hell breaks loose. A strange tale, filled with outrageous erotic oddities, that finally returns to print after years of infamy.

"An adventure novel told by a sex-bent male mini-pygmy. This is an accomplishment of which anybody may be proud."

—Philip José Farmer

TITIAN BERESFORD

The Wicked Hand   **$5.95/343-0**

With a special Introduction by *Leg Show*'s Dian Hanson. A collection of fanciful fetishistic tales featuring the absolute subjugation of men by lovely, domineering women. From Japan and Germany to the American heartland—these stories uncover the other side of the "weaker sex."

CHARISSE VAN DER LYN

Sex on the Net   **$5.95/399-6**

Electrifying erotica from one of the Internet's hottest and most widely read authors. Encounters of all kinds—straight, lesbian, dominant/submissive and all sorts of extreme passions—are explored in thrilling detail. Discover what's turning on hackers from coast to coast!

STANLEY CARTEN

Naughty Message   **$5.95/333-3**

Wesley Arthur, a withdrawn computer engineer, discovers a lascivious message on his answering machine. Aroused beyond his wildest dreams by the acts described, Wesley becomes obsessed with tracking down the woman behind the seductive voice. His search takes him through phone sex services, strip clubs and no-tell motels—and finally to his randy reward....

CAROLE REMY

Beauty of the Beast   **$5.95/332-5**

A shocking tell-all, written from the point-of-view of a prize-winning reporter. And what reporting she does! All the secrets of an uninhibited life are revealed, and each lusty tableau is painted in glowing colors. Join in on her scandalous adventures—and reap the rewards of her extensive background in Erotic Affairs!

SIDNEY ST. JAMES

Rive Gauche $5.95/317-1

Decadence and debauchery among the doomed artists in the Latin Quarter, Paris circa 1920. Expatriate bohemians couple with abandon—before eventually abandoning their ambitions amidst the intoxicating temptations waiting to be indulged in every bedroom. Finally, "creative impulse" takes on a whole new meaning for each lusty eccentric!

J. P. KANSAS

Andrea at the Center $5.95/324-4

Kidnapped! Lithe and lovely young Andrea is, without warning, whisked away to a distant retreat. Gradually, she is introduced to the ways of the Center, and soon becomes quite friendly with its other inhabitants—all of whom are learning to abandon all restraint! A big, brawling tale of total submission.

SARA H. FRENCH

Master of Timberland $5.95/327-9

"Welcome to Timberland Resort," he began. "We are delighted that you have come to serve us. And…be assured that we will require service of you in the strictest sense. Our discipline is the most demanding in the world. You will be trained here by the best. And now your new Masters will make their choices." A tale of sexual slavery at the ultimate paradise resort. One of our runaway bestsellers.

PAUL LITTLE

The Prisoner $5.95/330-9

Judge Black has built a secret room below a penitentiary, where he sentences the prisoners to hours of exhibition and torment while his friends watch. Judge Black's House of Corrections is equipped with one purpose in mind: to administer his own brand of rough justice!

All the Way $4.95/3023-7

Two excruciating novels from Paul Little in one hot volume! *Going All the Way* features an unhappy man who tries to purge himself of the memory of his lover with a series of quirky and uninhibited lovers. *Pushover* tells the story of a serial spanker and his celebrated exploits. These stories combine to make one of Little's most perfectly debauched titles.

Slave Island $4.95/3006-7

Lord Philbrock, a sadistic genius, has built a hidden paradise where captive females are forced into slavery. Cruise ships are waylaid, and the unsuspecting passengers put through Lord Philbrock's training. They are trained to accommodate the most bizarre sexual cravings of the rich, the famous, the pampered, and the perverted.

Chinese Justice $4.95/153-5

The notorious Paul Little indulges his penchant for discipline in these wild tales. *Chinese Justice* is already a classic—the story of the excruciating pleasures and delicious punishments inflicted on foreigners under the tyrannical leaders of the Boxer Rebellion.

TITIAN BERESFORD

Cinderella $4.95/024-5

A magical exploration of the full erotic potential of this fairy tale. Titian Beresford (*Nina Foxton, Judith Boston*) triumphs again with castle dungeons and tightly corseted ladies-in-waiting, naughty viscounts and impossibly cruel masturbatrixes—nearly every conceivable method of erotic torture is explored and described in lush, vivid detail. A fetishist's dream!

M A S Q U E R A D E

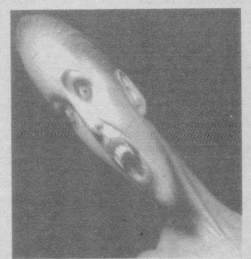

THE DARKER PASSIONS:

DRACULA

"The Transylvanian with fangs is a very sexy dude, and when you join his toothiness
with S/M fare, it's a winning combination...."
—*Michael Perkins*

A M A R A N T H A   K N I G H T

CHARLOTTE ROSE

A Dangerous Day $5.95/293-0

A new volume from the best-selling author who brought you the sensational *Women at Work* and *The Doctor Is In*. And if you thought the high-powered entanglements of her previous books were risky, wait until Rose takes you on a journey through the thrills of one dangerous day! A woman learns to let go—with the help of a mysterious and sexy stranger, who takes her places she has never been....

AMARANTHA KNIGHT

The Darker Passions: Dracula $5.95/326-0

From the realm of legend comes the grand beast of Eros, the famed and dreaded seducer and defiler of innocence. His name is Dracula, and no virgin is protected from his unspeakable ravishments. One by one he brings his victims to the ecstasy that will make them his forever. An acclaimed modern classic, and the first of Knight's "Darker Passions."

The Darker Passions: The Fall of the House of Usher $5.95/313-9

Two weary travelers arrive at the Usher home—a gloomy manse wherein they will find themselves faced with the dark secrets of desire. The Master and Mistress of the house indulge in every conceivable form of decadence, and are intent on initiating their guests into the many pleasures to be found in utter submission. But something is not quite right in the House of Usher, and the foundation of its dynasty begins to crack....

The Darker Passions: Dr. Jekyll and Mr. Hyde $5.95/227-2

It is a classic story, one of incredible, frightening transformations achieved through mysterious experiments. Now, Amarantha Knight—author of the popular erotic retelling of the Dracula legend—explores the steamy possibilities of a tale where no one is quite who they seem.

SARAH JACKSON

Sanctuary $5.95/318-X

Tales from the Middle Ages. *Sanctuary* explores both the unspeakable debauchery of court life and the unimaginable privations of monastic solitude, leading the voracious and the virtuous on a collision course that brings history to throbbing life. Bored royals and yearning clerics start fires sure to bring light to the darkest of ages.

ALIZARIN LAKE

The Instruments of the Passion $4.95/3010-5

All that remains is the diary of a young initiate, detailing the rituals of a mysterious cult institution known only as "Rossiter." Behind sinister walls, a beautiful woman performs an unending drama of pain and humiliation. Will she ever be satisfied...?

ANONYMOUS

School Days in Paris $5.95/325-2

A delicious duo of erotic awakenings. The rapturous chronicles of a well-spent youth! Few Universities provide the profound and pleasurable lessons one learns in after-hours study—particularly if one is young and bursting with promise, and lucky enough to have Paris as a playground.

Jennifer III $5.95/292-2

The further adventures of erotica's most daring heroine. Jennifer, the quintessential beautiful blonde, has a photographer's eye for detail—particularly details of the masculine variety! Jennifer lets nothing stand between her and her goal: total pleasure through sensual abandon.

Man With a Maid   **$4.95/307-4**
Over 80,000 copies in print! A classic of its genre, *Man with a Maid* tells an outrageous tale of desire, revenge, and submission.

Man With a Maid II   **$4.95/3071-7**
Jack's back! With the assistance of the perverse Alice, he embarks again on a trip through every erotic extreme. Jack leaves no one unsatisfied—least of all, himself, and Alice is always certain to outdo herself in her capacity to corrupt and control. An incendiary sequel!

Man With a Maid: The Conclusion   **$4.95/3013-X**
The final chapter in this saga of lust that has thrilled readers for decades. The adulterous woman who is corrected with enthusiasm and the clumsy maid who receives grueling guidance are just two who benefit from these lessons!

The Complete Erotic Reader   **$4.95/3063-6**
The very best in erotic writing together in a wicked collection sure to stimulate even the most jaded and "sophisticated" palates.

RHINOCEROS BOOKS

No Other Tribute   **Edited by Laura Antoniou**
A collection of stories sure to challenge Political Correctness in a way few have before, with tales of women kept in bondage to their lovers by their deepest passions. Love pushes these women beyond acceptable limits, rendering them helpless to deny the men and women they adore. Laura Antoniou brings together the most provocative women's writing in this companion volume to *By Her Subdued*.   **$6.95/294-9**

Flesh Fantastic   *Edited by Amarantha Knight*
Humans have long toyed with the idea of "playing God": creating life from nothingness, bringing Life to the inanimate. Now Amarantha Knight, author of the "Darker Passions" series, collects the very best stories exploring not only the allure of Creation, but the lust that may follow....   **$6.96/352-X**

Venus in Furs   *Leopold von Sacher-Masoch*
This classic 19th century novel is the first uncompromising exploration of the dominant/submissive relationship in literature. The alliance of Severin and Wanda epitomizes Sacher-Masoch's obsession with a cruel, controlling goddess and the urges that drive the man held in her thrall.   **$6.95/3089-X**

The Loving Dominant   *John Warren*
"Mentor"—as the author is known on the scene—is a longtime player in the dominance/submission scene, and he guides readers through this rarely seen world, and offers clear-eyed advice guaranteed to enlighten the most jaded erotic explorers. Mentor reveals the hidden basis of the D/S relationship: the care, trust and love between partners.   **$6.95/218-3**

Season of the Witch   *Jean Stine*
He committed an unforgivable crime, and and pays for it in ways that he never imagined. A rapist undergoes the ultimate punishment— transformation into the woman who was his target...   **$6.95/268-X**

GARY BOWEN

Diary of a Vampire   **$5.95/331-7**
"Gifted with a darkly sensual vision and a fresh voice, [Bowen] is a writer to watch out for."
                                                    —Cecilia Tan
The chilling, arousing, and ultimately moving memoirs of an undead—but all too human—soul. Rafael, a red-blooded male with an insatiable hunger for same, is the perfect antidote to the effete malcontents haunting bookstores today. A bold and brilliant vision, firmly rooted in past *and* present.

ANDREI CODRESCU

The Repentance of Lorraine $6.95/329-5

"His command of language is superb, his writing beautifully original, and his insights piercing." —*Harper's Magazine*

"One of our most prodigiously talented and magical writers."

—*New York Times Book Review*

From one of America's foremost writers and social commentators comes an early erotic romp. Hot on the heels of Codrescu's latest novel (*The Blood Countess*) comes the reissue of one of his first—the enchanting *Repentance of Lorraine*.

PHILIP JOSÉ FARMER

Flesh $6.95/303-1

One of Farmer's most infamous science fiction yarns. Space Commander Stagg explored the galaxies for 800 years, and could only hope that he would be welcomed home by an adoring—or at least *appreciative*—public. And upon his return, the hero Stagg is made the centerpiece of an incredible public ritual—one that will repeatedly take him to the heights of ecstasy, and inexorably drag him toward the depths of hell.

A Feast Unknown $6.95/276-0

"Sprawling, brawling, shocking, suspenseful, hilarious…"

—Theodore Sturgeon

Farmer's supreme anti-hero returns. *A Feast Unknown* begins in 1968, with Lord Grandrith's stunning statement: "I was conceived and born in 1888. Jack the Ripper was my father." Slowly, Lord Grandrith—armed with this belief—tells the story of his remarkable and unbridled life. Beginning with his discovery of the secret of immortality, Grandrith's tale proves him no raving lunatic—but something far more bizarre….

MICHAEL PERKINS

The Secret Record: Modern Erotic Literature $6.95/3039-3

Perkins, a renowned author and critic of sexually explicit fiction, surveys the field with authority and unique insight. Updated and revised to include the latest trends, tastes, and developments in this much-misunderstood genre.

GRANT ANTREWS

Submissions $6.95/207-8

Another stunning, sensitive tale from the author of *My Darling Dominatrix*. Once again, Antrews portrays the very special elements of the dominant/submissive relationship with restraint—this time with the story of a lonely man, a winning lottery ticket, and a demanding dominatrix.

SARA ADAMSON

"Ms. Adamson's friendly, conversational writing style perfectly couches what to some will be shocking material. Ms. Adamson creates a wonderfully diverse world of lesbian, gay, straight, bi and transgendered characters, all mixing delightfully in the melting pot of sadomasochism and planting the genre more firmly in the culture at large. I for one am cheering her on!" —Kate Bornstein

The Trainer $6.95/249-3

The long-awaited conclusion of Adamson's stunning Marketplace Trilogy! The ultimate underground sexual realm includes not only willing slaves, but the exquisite and demanding trainers who take submissives firmly in hand. And it is now the time for these mentors to lay bare the desires that compelled them to become the ultimate figures of erotic authority.

THE SLAVE

S A R A A D A M S O N

"...perverse SM Erotica, mixing hetero and
homosexuality in the tradition of Anne
Rice's **Beauty** series."
—*Lambda Book Report*

$6.95 (CANADA $7.95) • RHINOCEROS BOOKS

The Slave $6.95/173-X

The second volume in the "Marketplace" trilogy. *The Slave* covers the experience of one exceptionally talented submissive who longs to join the ranks of those who have proven themselves worthy of entry into the Marketplace. But the price, while delicious, is staggeringly high....

The Marketplace $6.95/3096-2

"Merchandise does not come easily to the Marketplace.... They haunt the clubs and the organizations, their need so real and desperate that they exude sensual tension when they glide through the crowds. Some of them are so ripe that they intimidate the poseurs, the weekend sadists and the furtive dilettantes who are so endemic to that world. And they never stop asking where we are found..."

ROSEBUD BOOKS

The Rosebud Reader $5.95/319-8

Rosebud Books—the hottest-selling line of lesbian erotica available—here collects the very best of the best. Rosebud has contributed greatly to the burgeoning genre of lesbian erotica—to the point that authors like Lindsay Welsh, Aarona Griffin and Valentina Cilescu are among the hottest and most closely watched names in lesbian and gay publishing. Here are the finest moments from Rosebud's contemporary classics.

LINDSAY WELSH

Provincetown Summer $5.95/362-7

"These tales are extremely enjoyable...reading may be interrupted by increased passion." —*Perception*

This completely original collection is devoted exclusively to white-hot desire between women. From the casual encounters of women on the prowl to the enduring erotic bonds between old lovers, the women of *Provincetown Summer* will set your senses on fire! A nationally best-selling title.

A Victorian Romance $5.95/365-1

Lust-letters from the road. A young Englishwoman realizes her dream—a trip abroad under the guidance of her eccentric maiden aunt. Soon the young but blossoming Elaine comes to discover her own sexual talents, as a hot-blooded Parisian named Madelaine takes her Sapphic education in hand.

A Circle of Friends $4.95/250-7

The author of the nationally best-selling *Provincetown Summer* returns with the story of a remarkable group of women. Slowly, the women pair off to explore all the possibilities of lesbian passion, until finally it seems that there is nothing and no one they have not dabbled in.

EDITED BY LAURA ANTONIOU

"...a great new collection of fiction by and about SM dykes."
—*SKIN TWO*

Leatherwomen $4.95/3095-4

A groundbreaking anthology. These fantasies, from the pens of new or emerging authors, break every rule imposed on women's fantasies. The hottest stories from some of today's newest writers make this an unforgettable exploration of the female libido.

Leatherwomen II $4.95/229-9

Once again, Laura Antoniou turned a discerning eye to the writing of women on the edge—resulting in a second collection sure to ignite libidinal flames in any reader. Leave taboos behind, and be ready to speak the unspeakable—because these Leatherwomen know no limits...

ORDERING IS EASY!

MC/VISA orders can be placed by calling our toll-free number

PHONE 800 375-2356/FAX 212 986-7355

or mail the coupon below to:

MASQUERADE BOOKS
DEPT. X74A, 801 SECOND AVENUE, NY, NY 10017

BUY ANY FOUR BOOKS AND CHOOSE ONE ADDITIONAL BOOK, OF EQUAL OR LESSER VALUE, AS YOUR FREE GIFT.

QTY.	TITLE	NO.	PRICE
			FREE
			FREE

X74A

SUBTOTAL

POSTAGE and HANDLING

We Never Sell, Give or Trade Any Customer's Name.

TOTAL

In the U.S., please add $1.50 for the first book and 75¢ for each additional book; in Canada, add $2.00 for the first book and $1.25 for each additional book. Foreign countries: add $4.00 for the first book and $2.00 for each additional book. No C.O.D. orders. Please make all checks payable to Masquerade Books. Payable in U.S. currency only. New York state residents add 8¼% sales tax. Please allow 4-6 weeks delivery.

NAME _____

ADDRESS _____

CITY _____ STATE _____ ZIP _____

TEL ( ) _____

PAYMENT: ☐ CHECK ☐ MONEY ORDER ☐ VISA ☐ MC

CARD NO. _____ EXP. DATE _____